Time to Roll

Also by Jamie Sumner

Roll with It
Tune It Out
One Kid's Trash
The Summer of June

Time to Roll

JAMIE SUMNER

ATHENEUM BOOKS FOR YOUNG READERS
New York London Toronto Sydney New Delhi

atheneum

ATHENEUM BOOKS FOR YOUNG READERS

An imprint of Simon & Schuster Children's Publishing Division

1230 Avenue of the Americas, New York, New York 10020

Text © 2023 by Jamie Sumner

Jacket illustration © 2023 by Amy Marie Stadelmann

Jacket design by Karyn Lee © 2023 by Simon & Schuster, Inc.

For information about special discounts for bulk purchases, please contact Simon & Schuster Special Sales at 1-866-506-1949 or business@simonandschuster.com.

The Simon & Schuster Speakers Bureau can bring authors to your live event. For more information or to book an event, contact the Simon & Schuster Speakers Bureau at 1-866-248-3049 or visit our website at www.simonspeakers.com.

Interior design by Karyn Lee

The text for this book was set in Adobe Garamond Pro.

Manufactured in the United States of America

0223 FFG

First Edition

10 9 8 7 6 5 4 3 2 1

Library of Congress Cataloging-in-Publication Data

Names: Sumner, Jamie, author.

Title: Time to roll / Jamie Sumner.

Description: First edition. | New York : Atheneum Books for Young Readers, 2023. | Audience: Ages 10 Up. | Summary: When thirteen-year-old Ellie reluctantly agrees to enter a beauty pageant with her best friend Coralee, the director seems determined to feature Ellie and her wheelchair, so she must find a way to participate on her own terms, all while saving her friendship and forming a better relationship with her divorced dad.

Identifiers: LCCN 2022004260 | ISBN 9781665918596 (hardcover) | ISBN 9781665918619 (ebook)

Subjects: CYAC: People with disabilities—Fiction. | Cerebral palsy—Fiction. | Best friends—Fiction. | Friendship—Fiction. | Beauty contests—Fiction. | Family life—Fiction. | Fathers and daughters—Fiction.

Classification: LCC PZ7.1.S8545 Ti 2023 | DDC [Fic]—dc23

LC record available at https://lccn.loc.gov/2022004260

For Cora—a fierce beauty

1

Happily Ever After

Peach is not my color. And silk is *definitely* not my fab-ric. But what am I going to do—boycott my own mother's wedding? Pull a runaway bride, except it would be a run-away maid of honor? I'd be hightailing it out of here with flower petals trailing from my wheels. Actually, that doesn't sound half bad. I wipe a bead of sweat from my forehead with the handkerchief Mema tucked into my bouquet. It's about five thousand degrees too hot for nuptials.

"Okay, wedding party, one more shot and then we're *golden*!" Coralee shouts from where she crouches on her knees in the sand by the lake. She's trying her hand at photography. Apparently, that's the quadruple threat in her plan to take over the world and become a famous celebrity.

Now she can add photographer to her actor/singer/dancer résumé. Pretty soon, she's going to over-qualify herself right out of the running. But that's just my personal opinion, which I do not plan to tell my best friend. Coralee does not take criticism well. In fact, she could probably handle a live scorpion better than one word about her outfit, hair, or singing ability. One time, during a rehearsal for the spring musical at school, the chorus director told her to "maybe tone it down a bit," and she snapped, "Excuse me? Do you even *want* people to come to this show?"

"Ellie, it's not the zombie apocalypse." She sighs. "Smile like you think somebody's *not* about to eat your face."

I blink in the hot Oklahoma sun. "Shut it, Coralee." I give her my sweetest, most evil grin.

"Baby, you need a break?" Mom leans down from her spot two steps above me in the gazebo and tucks my hair behind my ear. Her cheeks are rosy from heat and happiness. Mema made both our dresses, but hers suits her to a T. It's cream silk and sleeveless and stops at her knees. On anybody else it'd be plain, but on Mom it is perfection. I smile up at her, and she winks just as Coralee snaps a picture.

"Got it!" Coralee yells. "That's a wrap, people. Now go get hitched!"

"There's still time to make a run for it," Hutch whispers to both of us. Coaching middle school football camp the last couple of weeks, since school ended, has given him a fierce farmer's tan, but he still looks handsome in his white button-down shirt with the sleeves rolled up. His tie is peach, like my dress. When Mom punches him in the shoulder, he grins and she blushes and I rock back on my wheels so I do not have to watch yet another display of affection. I love them both. I do. And it is their wedding day. But come *on*. They're worse than middle schoolers.

Behind us, up near the tree line, gravel crunches and car doors slam. "Come on, let's go hide." Mom nudges my knee with hers before letting me take the lead down the dirt path to the tent they've set up by the water for the reception.

When Hutch and Mom started getting serious, I thought it might be weird having my gym teacher around all the time. But then it just . . . wasn't. My world expanded to three after it being just Mom and me for so long. After a while I couldn't even remember what it was like without Hutch mowing the lawn and challenging me to knuckle-cracking contests and stepping on his own two feet while Mom tried to teach him to line dance in our teeny tiny kitchen.

So when he stopped by the trailer while Mom was at the grocery store one afternoon and asked if we could have a chat out on the porch, I knew what was coming. All the most important conversations happen on the porch. It's the place you go to iron out the wrinkles with your people. When you live in extra-close quarters like we do, you need a spot of neutral territory.

Hutch paced the length of the porch for about ten minutes until he bumped his head on the bug zapper and retreated to the rocking couch across from me. We sat without talking for so long that I started doing mini push-ups in my wheelchair to have something to do.

"You're getting good at those," he said, finally.

I did my best Schwarzenegger impression. "Yeah, I'm gonna get ripped."

He gave me a shaky laugh. "I guess I should take credit when you become a world-famous bodybuilder."

I shook my head. Hutch has been the best physical therapist I've ever had. But I couldn't let it go to his head. "It's twenty percent coaching, eighty percent sheer will-power." I patted his arm. "You're all right, though. My PT back in Nashville had me take ten steps in the gait trainer and call it a day. Pretty sure she thought any kind of exercise that made me stronger *in* my chair was a step back. Pun intended."

Crickets. Man, if he didn't get on with it soon, I'd have to propose to him myself.

"I hope"—he stopped and cleared his throat—"I might become more to you than just your PT."

"You're a champ at lawn care." I couldn't help myself.

"That too, but also, I mean. . . ." He stood and started pacing again. "Your mom and I have been spending a lot of time together, and when two people like to spend time together and, um, like each other like your mom and I do, we . . ." He trailed off, looking lost. "Ellie, do you know what I'm trying to say?"

"Yeah, sure. You like Mom and Mom likes you and you want to be a part of our lives permanently."

He nodded, visibly relieved.

"Like me and Bert and Coralee. Best friends, right?"

He rubbed both hands over his face like he wished he could peel it right off. I chuckled and surrendered. There's only so much tween torture a man can take.

"I'm *kidding*. You want to marry my mom, right?"

He collapsed onto the rocking couch, sending it squeaking back and forth. "*Yes.* I want to be part of your family in whatever way you will let me, because I think you're pretty cool. Slightly wicked with what you just did there, but also cool and stubborn and an incredible baker, and I'd be honored if you'd let me into your inner circle."

I looked him up and down, his shaved head shiny in the early spring air, his knee bouncing the same way mine does when I'm nervous, and I nodded.

"Okay."

"Okay?"

"Yeah, okay. We'll let you in."

He heaved a huge sigh and pulled out two glazed tea cakes from Mimi's Café in town that he must've stashed out here earlier. Total bribery, but I didn't care. I wonder if I still would have gotten one if I'd said no. Probably. Hutch is that kind of guy.

"Hey, man, the war's not over yet. You've still got to get Mom to say yes."

"Are you kidding?" he said, grinning and taking a huge bite of pastry. "After this, proposing to Alice will be a piece of cake."

"Speaking of cake," I said, and pointed to a sizable crumb stuck to his chin.

Looking over at him now, under the tent with his arm over Mom's shoulder, I have no doubt I made the right decision. I don't remember what it was like before my real dad left. I was just a baby. But whatever it was like, it couldn't have been as good. Because how could you have this and ever let it go?

Dad. My stomach clenches hard like a sinkhole swallowing up all the good vibes. I roll to the edge of the tent and look out over the calm water. I *cannot* and *will not* think about him right now. That's what tomorrow's for. And every day after that for the next month.

"Girl!" Coralee shouts with her camera held over her head like a trophy. "You look awesome in these!"

I'm not great with compliments, so I'm still trying to figure out what to say to that when she adds, "I rock at this picture-taking thing." I smack her arm, but it's good. Coralee is distracting. She brings me back to the present— to the moment I get to watch my mom on the happiest day of her life, second only to when she had me, of course.

2

The First Law of Motion

"I thought Pastor Clark was going to pass out right in the middle of the vows." Mema chuckles and hands me a plate of barbecued pork and beans. They had it catered from the new place, Moe's, whose slogan is "We go in whole hog!" I pick up a plastic fork, hoping that doesn't mean I'm about to eat a tail.

Mema didn't cry during the ceremony like I thought she would. Instead she sat next to Grandpa with her hand on his knee and nodded her head like, *It's about time.* It's hard to believe it was just a year ago that she and Grandpa moved into the condo at Autumn Leaves so they could get more care for his Alzheimer's. I think it might have been the only time in her life she's ever let somebody help her.

"That man better hydrate," she says, eyeing Pastor Clark, whose periwinkle bow tie is bobbing up and down as he coughs over by the gift table. "I did *not* tithe for over two decades to watch him collapse from heatstroke at my daughter's wedding." I laugh into my beans. Condo life hasn't softened her one bit. She's still tough as nails.

"Lord! What happened to Evy?" Grandpa shouts, before we can shush him. He's gotten thinner over the past year. His starched shirt hangs off him like a hanger. But his voice works just fine.

All of us, including Coralee and my other best friend, Bert, sneak glances at the table to our right, where Mrs. Evelyn Crebold sits with her husband, Shane. Her lips are painted neon orange, and they are stretched into a mile-wide grimace as she holds a piece of pork up to the light like she's checking for a stray hair. I hope she gets the tail.

"Poor woman looks like she's been embalmed!" Grandpa yells.

Mom covers her mouth to stifle a laugh.

Coralee leans in to whisper. She's changed into an electric-blue sequined dress, with sleeves so puffy they almost reach her ears. "Rumor has it, when *Mr.* Crebold started coming home late every Thursday night with pastries from Mimi's, *Mrs.* Crebold got it in her head he was having an affair. So she went and got herself a face-lift." Coralee circles her own face for emphasis. "Turns out, Thursday is discount day at Mimi's. Here he was trying to save money and she went and spent all their savings on a nip and tuck!"

Bert shakes his head. "Faces are meant to succumb to gravitational forces like everything else. It's Newton's first law of motion." He takes a bite of barbecue and then adds, "To fight it is to fight nature." Despite his best efforts with a water and comb, his black hair sticks up at all angles, doing a pretty good job of defying gravity. But it would be useless to point that out. Just like you don't criticize Coralee, you don't argue facts with Bert.

I glance back over at Evy. I remember how she patted my head at the Christmas Eve service last year when we first moved here and how she *continues* to pat my head every time she sees me, like I'm a pet, not a person. Then I whisper, *not* very quietly, "She looks like someone pulled her hair back and then just kept pulling."

Coralee slaps the table, and Hutch chokes on his lemonade. Bert nods, granting my point. But Mema says, "No, ma'am," shaking her head at me while crumbling cornbread into Grandpa's beans. "We do not judge others. She can do whatever she wants. It's her face and *none* of our business."

"But—"

"No buts," Mom says. "When we leave tomorrow, I expect you to be on your best behavior. None of this attitude."

I push my plate away, appetite gone. Mom must see the fear flicker across my face at the thought of tomorrow, because she softens and lays her hand over mine. Her wedding ring with its tiny diamond sparkles in the afternoon light.

"You can still come, you know."

I shake my head. "No. No way am I going on your honeymoon with you. I have no interest in riding around in an RV for a month, trailing Route 66 across the state of Oklahoma." I pull my hand back. "I want to spend the summer with my friends."

"We'll keep her in line, *Mrs. Hutchinson*," Coralee says, crossing her heart. I kick her under the table.

"It's still Alice Cowan, Coralee," Mom reminds her. "You know I'm keeping my name."

"Darn right she is!" Grandpa thumps his fist on the table and we all freeze, waiting to see if this is the kind of anger that passes like a wave or hits like a hurricane. "Cowan is a mighty fine name," he adds, and winks at me, just like Mom does. Everybody breathes again.

"All I'm saying, honey," Mom says, ignoring the caterer, who is waving her arms from across the tent so that Mom and Hutch will come cut the cake, "is that it's not too late to change your mind."

I roll back from the table. "Come on. I didn't make a four-tiered coconut cake with coconut custard and fondant sunflowers for nothing."

When nobody moves, I turn away from all of them and roll over the uneven grass toward the cake, stopping only long enough to stare pointedly at Evy until she scoots her chair closer to the table so I can wheel by.

Mom's wrong. Like Bert's gravitational forces, there are already too many parts and people in motion. It's way too late to change my mind.

3

A Room of One's Own

The thing about cerebral palsy is that I've lived with it every day of my life, so I'm used to it. But to the rest of the world, it's a surprise. And not usually a good one. It's like if you were really hoping for a bike for your birthday, but got a thousand-piece puzzle instead. Your parents *really* want you to be open-minded about the puzzle, so you fake a smile. All you can think about, though, is how fast you could be going on your bike right now.

That's the face my father makes when I open the door to the trailer the morning after Mom's wedding. He'd rather be on a bike, and he's wondering how in the world he got stuck with this puzzle. Back at you, Dad.

"Ellie! Hello!" he booms.

I wince. We aren't on a conference call. He's not in the courtroom. And I am not hard of hearing. He can just . . . talk. This better not be his standard volume the entire month he's here to stay with me while Mom and Hutch go on their honeymoon, or I'm going to need some earplugs. And miles of personal space.

"Hi, Dad."

Mom walks up behind me. "Greg."

"Alice."

That's it. Just "Greg." "Alice." So much is being lobbed back and forth in the silence, though, that I roll back. In my head I hear video game noises as Mom racks up the points. Dad already looks like he's ready to run in the opposite direction. No surprise there.

"Ellie! It's so nice to see you in the flesh again!" Meg, my stepmother, dives between Dad and the door like a stealth bomber and grabs me in a tight squeeze. She's a hugger. And a hand holder. And a high-fiver. But she's never patted my head, so I say, "Hi, Meg," when she finally releases me to call over her shoulder to Finn and Patrick, my stepbrothers, who are engaged in some sort of kung fu battle to the death in the driveway.

At her whistle, they barrel in, already covered in dust. If Mema still lived here, she'd smile and then make them clean every last bit of it up. It might be a trailer, but it is a *clean* trailer. *Greg* and *Meg* don't seem to notice.

"Boys, say hi to your sister," Meg orders, and I think, *Shouldn't my dad be the one getting them to talk to me?*

"Hi," Patrick says. He's six and has grown tall enough since the last time I saw him to look me in the eye when I'm in my chair. To his credit, he does.

"Hi!" Finn parrots, walking backward around me in a big circle. He's four and has what looks to be a grape Jolly Rancher stuck in his blond curls. He got the hair from Meg. Both boys have it. Which leaves me the odd one out on every level.

"Umm, hey, kid," I say to Finn when he finally stops his backward dance.

"Hey, El! I'm practicing my *moon* dance."

"It's moonwalk, dummy," Patrick says, and shoves him. Finn falls forward into me, knocking my chair sideways so my shoulder and elbow bump into the wall.

"That is *enough!*" Dad shouts like both boys just sucker punched me. It wasn't that big of a deal. It didn't even hurt. "No roughhousing around Ellie!"

I curl my elbows into my sides as they mumble, "Sorry." I'd *keep* curling into myself if I could, until I disappear. Dad is already treating me like he does every time they visit or I go back to Nashville with Mom for a doctor's appointment—like any little bump will break me. In case

15

I'd forgotten, it's a giant red flashing sign that he doesn't know me at all.

Just then Hutch comes around the corner, humming some country song way off-key, and I want a do-over. I want to go with him and Mom in the RV. Anything to not be left here with these people.

"Crepes soon. Right, kiddo?" Mom whispers, leaning over me so I catch the smell of her—aloe lotion and lavender shampoo. I cough once so my voice is steady.

"Yeah, breakfast in five," I reply, and reverse back down the hallway until I can disappear into the safety of the kitchen.

Dear Joy the Baker,

I'm not sure if "Joy the Baker" is your official title, like the "Queen of England" or "Oscar the Grouch," but I'm going with it.

First off, you rock. Seriously. I have already made my mom swear to take me to your Bakehouse in New Orleans so I can do a workshop for my sixteenth birthday. Also, your cat Tron is so cute. Even my mema agrees, and she's the one who says cats basically exist to prove that some things in nature have no purpose.

Second, I apologize for what I am about to say: I thought French Southern cuisine was for everybody, but it is decidedly not. I made your lemon poppy-seed crepes with the blueberry curd for my stepmother (who is not wicked) and stepbrothers (who aren't either) and father (who might be). All my stepbrothers said was "Why are these pancakes so flat?" And my stepmother couldn't even try them because she is allergic to poppy seeds. How would I know? And though my dad tried a few bites, apparently he's not into "sweets for breakfast." Again, how would I know?

Anyway, your whole thing is "you do you," so I'm going to make this recipe again because I loved it. But next time I'll try to pick a more appreciative crowd. And if they don't like it either? Hey, more for me, right?

Give Tron a kiss for me.

All my best,

Ellie the Baker-in-Training

"I'm sorry again about the poppy seeds," I tell Meg as she helps me clear the almost-full plates from the kitchen table. The boys are already out back playing hide-and-seek in the garden.

"No, *I'm* sorry! They looked beautiful." She puts a hand on my shoulder. "They really did." She used the same voice on Finn when he came in to show her his favorite rock from the yard. I push back from the sink, dripping soapsuds all over my white T-shirt and the floor.

"Yeah, well, next time." Why did I say that? That implies I'm going to try this whole disastrous experiment again. Bert once told me the definition of insanity is repeating the same thing and expecting different results. I'm toeing the line.

The thing is, it should have gone perfectly. I made the crepe batter and the blueberry curd last night, because I knew my nerves would be frazzled before they got here. The only reason I chose crepes in the first place was because Dad gave me the expensive nonstick pans for my birthday this year and I wanted him to see me use them! He didn't even notice.

I wheel out of the kitchen, through the dining-room-slash-living-room, down the hall, and into the bathroom, where I lock myself in. Forget pans. The best gift I've ever been given was this room—a fully renovated, wheelchair-accessible bathroom of my very own. Hutch did the demolition himself. He let me take a few swings at the drywall with the sledgehammer. When I rolled through

18

the hole we made out into the sunlight, I was covered in drywall dust and Mom was none too pleased. But there is nothing, I repeat *nothing*, as satisfying as blasting through walls that were made to hold you back.

I study myself in the mirror in my very own bathroom with the roll-in shower and the low cabinets and the motion-sensor faucets over the sink. A constellation of freckles stretches over my nose and cheeks. My brown hair falls past my shoulders, longer than it's ever been, and straight as a pin like always.

I squint. You always see characters in movies and books with "violet" or "cerulean" or "emerald" eyes. Mine are just plain old blue. But they have spent the last year crinkling with laughter over checkers tournaments with Mema and Grandpa and peering at the replica of Eufaula's tree-lined streets in Bert's tiny town that he built in his shed and crying while chopping onions for the turkey and dressing I made for Thanksgiving while Coralee sat on the kitchen table and sang Reba McEntire songs. My ordinary eyes have seen so much over the past year and a half since we moved here. But they've only spent a heartbeat of time taking in Dad and his *other* family. Why did I think we could do this? After a handful of visits here? Why did I think we could mesh like people do when they *want* to know each other?

19

Maybe I can set up a barricade? I'll stay in this bathroom for the next thirty days. Bert can smuggle me in some food from his parents' grocery store. Coralee can be in charge of clothing and toiletries. I'll even let her select a few outfits, sequins and all.

"Ellie?" Mom knocks lightly. She does not try the handle. She respects my personal space. "We're leaving, baby. Can you come out and say bye?" Her voice breaks on "bye." My reflection in the mirror goes blurry. I flush the toilet so she won't think I was hiding and then open the door.

She takes a good long look at my splotchy cheeks and sinks down in the hallway with her legs stretched out and her back up against the wall. "That's it. I'm not going."

"*Mom*, it's your honeymoon. You have to go."

"Nope." She crosses her arms. "You should know better than anyone that if you don't like a rule, you change it. Honeymoons are stupid. I'm too old to spend a month in an RV. I'm staying home."

She says she's old, but she looks a decade younger than she did not so long ago, when she spent most of her time waiting for me to have another seizure or worrying about the day Mema wouldn't be able to take care of Grandpa on her own. But it's been *years* since I've had a seizure. The doctor even officially cleared me off my meds. And

Grandpa is safe and sound with Mema at Autumn Leaves. Mom can't use us as an excuse.

Mom needs to take this trip for her.

"Time to kick you out of the nest, little chick." I put my hands on my knees and bend down so our faces are inches apart. "Go. On. Your. Honeymoon. You. Dope."

She leans forward until our noses touch.

"Only if you play the Lotto."

I sit back. "*Mom*. No."

The Lotto is a result of Mom's childhood spent reading one too many Baby-Sitters Club books. Part of the agreement of her leaving me alone—oh wait, I mean with *Dad*—to go on this trip was that I would participate in the Cowan Family Lotto, which consists of a jar on my bedside table filled with Ping-Pong balls numbered one through ten. The numbers go along with a list Mom made, entitled, you guessed it, *The Cowan Family Lotto*. Items include:

1. Smell something new.
2. Taste something new.
3. Hear something new.
4. See something new.
5. Hug someone.
6. Write to your mother.

7. Wiggle your toes, wiggle your fingers, wiggle your eyebrows. SMILE.
8. Tell a joke.
9. Imagine your favorite place.
10. Write to your mother.

Every day I'm supposed to draw a ball out of the jar and whatever number it is, I have to do that thing on the list. Bert is incredibly bothered that she put *Write to your mother* twice. He says she's skewing the odds. I told him that was her point.

A door slams. Outside, the boys yell. Overhead, squirrels chase each other, their claws scritch-scratching on the tin roof. The world is moving on, with or without us.

I hold out my hand to her.

"I promise to do the Lotto if you promise to go on this trip."

She takes my hand and I pull her up.

"And promise to try to be nice to your dad, too?"

He's the one who should be made to promise things, I think as I roll backward down the hall while she follows. But I paste on a smirk instead and say, "One step at a time, Mom. One step at a time."

Before I know it, we are through the open front door and I am waving while they pull away. My arm might as well weigh a thousand pounds with the effort of this goodbye. I let it drop like a hammer onto my lap, where it sits as heavy as my heart. Her leaving is too fast. I can already feel how slow her coming back will be. I watch the silver side of the RV glinting in the sunlight all the way to the end of the gravel road until it disappears around the corner, carrying half my family with it. The other half lives in a condo at Autumn Leaves. These people I'm left with, shuffling back inside and arguing over bologna versus turkey sandwiches for lunch, they're not family. They are placeholders. I gulp in the air that's too hot for the beginning of June. It's going to be four very long weeks.

4

A Massively Fantastic Distraction

"No, Eric, I can't pull up the file right now. Why? Because I am on *sabbatical*." Dad paces the porch, yelling. His phone voice, that booming conference-call yell, has stunned the birds and squirrels and crickets into silence. The dust's barely settled from Mom and Hutch's departure and he has already hit max volume. He makes small, tight laps and shouts at nothing. "The month of June is off-limits. You know this! Ask Karen or any of the other four partners. Yes. Yes. Fine." He sighs and presses a button on his headset. Mission control, signing off. Only then does he spot me, at the bottom of the porch ramp.

"Hey, kiddo. Lunch isn't ready yet. Want to go for a walk? Er—" He scratches his head. I wait it out. "A stroll?"

I think of Mom, how she wants me to "try."

"Yeah, I guess."

We take the dirt path between Coralee's grandparents' trailer and ours, because it's not gravel and I can wheel myself. No way am I letting Dad push me. The path winds between thick pines and what I now know are blackjack oaks, thanks to Bert's tiny town and encyclopedic knowledge of basically everything. The air is thick with the sticky cinnamon scent of sun-warmed sap. Dad and I don't talk, which is fine by me.

When the path meets up with Route 9, Dad turns in a full circle, looking up and down the road. There's nothing for miles in any direction but blue sky and red earth.

"Which way?" he asks.

I swallow a joke about a "fork in the road" and turn left. "This way's Number Nine landing and the lake. Keep going and you eventually hit the bridge and cross into town." I turn right. "There's not much this way." *But it's where Mom went,* I think. "I vote right."

We go right, dirt kicking up under my wheels and his impossibly white sneakers. I can feel the sun calling *all* the freckles on my cheeks out to play, but I don't want to turn back just yet. This awkward silence is better than the loud chaos waiting for me back at the trailer.

Dad clears his throat. Oh boy, here we go. "You know, I'm glad we're going to get this time together, Ellie."

I make a noncommittal *mm-hmm* sound and pick up the pace.

"When you come to Nashville, you're always so busy with appointments, and I've got work. And when we visit you here, we only get to see you in bits and pieces while we travel back and forth from the motel. This will be good, all of us under one roof. The perfect vacation." He nods, satisfied. Case closed. My cheeks burn and this time it's from anger, not the heat. He treats people like things to be managed.

"Yeah. So glad Mom found the love of her life so you could take a *vacation*." I hear Mom's voice in my head: *Enough with the snark, Ellie.* But Mom's not here. My buffer has left me. I can say whatever I want.

I look up at Dad, ready for a fight. A fight would feel good right now. Mema always says it's better to air out your dirty laundry before it has a chance to stink up the place. He squints at the sun, avoiding my eyes. "Lunch'll be ready soon. We'd better turn around."

Right. Dad can yell at co-workers and his own two *real* kids, but when it comes to me, his policy has always been "less is more." Unless less is just . . . less.

◇ ◇ ◇

My phone starts belching at eight p.m. on the dot. It's my ringtone for Mom, a joke that I find even more hilarious because Mom hates it so much. I let it belch a few seconds longer before I pick up, because it freaks me out how desperately I need to hear Mom's voice. This isn't me. I'm not a needy kid. I am the *opposite* of a needy kid. I am fully self-sufficient.

"Mom, you've been gone less than twelve hours."

"I know, baby, but I wanted to call, at least the first night. I wanted to see how you all were settling in. Emails only from here on out, I promise." Her voice is exactly how I remember it, which makes sense, since I just heard it this morning. *Get it together, Ellie.*

"I'm fine. We're fine."

"Did you eat the leftovers from Moe's?"

"Yeah, we ate them." *We,* ick. Dad and I should never be a "we." Mom and I are supposed to be the "we."

"Good, good. There must be at least fifteen pounds of pork left over in the fridge." She laughs. She's making small talk, with *me,* her one and only daughter. We don't know how to do the phone thing. We've never been separated long enough to learn.

A fire crackles in the background on her end. "Where are you guys?"

"We decided to stop and camp just down the road at the Lake Eufaula State Park. I've never been here all the years we've visited! I rode a horse. Can you believe it? He's called Sparky, and he rubbed my leg up against every tree on the trail. Jim thinks he sensed my fear and was trying to brush me off."

"You *would* annoy a horse," I say, but I'm smiling. Mom is terrified of big animals. She doesn't even like goldendoodles. I hope Hutch took pictures. I still can't get used to the fact that she calls him by his first name. He is *so* not a Jim. He was Coach Hutchinson first and then just Hutch, and Hutch he shall remain, to me at least.

"So if *I* were playing the Lotto, that'd be my number four. 'See something new.' I never thought I'd *see* the day I'd ride a horse."

"Ha ha. Cross number eight off the list too: 'Tell a joke.' Though that was so bad I'm not even sure it counts."

"You tell me one, then," Mom asks, ignoring my sass, per usual. The longer I talk to her, the more my room fades around me and I can see her, sitting by a fire in the woods with her bare feet up on a rock, toes painted bright red for the wedding. The picture hurts because I'm not in it.

"Okay, one joke for the road, and then I gotta go. Off to get my beauty sleep. Knock knock."

"Who's there?" she asks.

"Wheelie."

"Wheelie who?"

"You *wheelie* want to ask me that while I'm in this chair?"

Mom chuckles. "Oh, Ellie."

"What? I thought that one was *wheelie* good."

"I love you, El."

"Love you, too."

"Sleep tight," she adds. Neither one of us wants to hang up.

"Yeah, you too. Don't let the mutant campfire bugs bite."

"Thanks for *that* right before I go to bed."

"Anytime."

"Night, baby girl," she whispers.

"Night, Mom."

I wait for the click. Then I sit in the dark, pretending I can hear the sound of a crackling fire.

"Pssst. *Psssst.*"

The following morning I am lying in the corner of my room on the square of pressed-down carpet that is all I have left of Mema's sewing machine. I do this from time to time when I miss them living here. The room is mine all mine now, which I should be happy about. Mom and I redecorated—painted the brown oak-paneled walls bright white and bought the softest blue comforter and cushiest mattress we could find. When I sleep, I like it to feel like I am resting on a cloud. But right now, I'd lie on a bed of nails to have Mema and Grandpa back here.

"Pssssssssst."

"I know you're out there, Coralee," I yell up through the closed window. "You can come around to the front door. It's unlocked."

Less than a minute later, Coralee is sitting cross-legged on my floor in a pair of neon-yellow shorts and a matching neon sports bra. She looks like a highlighter.

"Why didn't you just text?" I ask.

"Because I knew you'd be in a funk with your mom abandoning you and you'd probably ignore me."

I push myself up and pull my legs toward me so they cross like hers, our knees touching. My hamstrings are tight. They burn as they stretch.

"She didn't abandon me."

Coralee waves her hand in the air, like my words are immaterial.

"Yeah, yeah. You love her. She loves you. This is a growing period for you both. Whatever."

I elbow her in the ribs.

"My *point* is," she says, rubbing her side, "that I have come with a massively fantastic, be-all and end-all distraction for you." Cue her jazz hands. Her nails are yellow too.

"Nope."

She drops her hands.

"What do you mean, 'nope'? You don't even know what it is yet."

"Doesn't matter. I'm not in the mood." I pick at a nubby piece of carpet and then flatten it down again so the sewing-machine square will remain.

"Right. You'd rather sit here and feel sorry for yourself. Maybe slink off to the kitchen and whip up a batch of 'I regret my life choices' chocolate chip cookies."

"You know, that's not a bad idea."

"Girl! *No.*" Coralee punches me in the shoulder, *way* harder than I poked her in the ribs. "I am not going to let you rot away in this room for the next month. We are getting *out.*"

"Out where?" Okay, I'm a little curious.

Coralee crosses her arms like she knows she's won, which she totally has not. And then she pulls out a folded piece of paper from her fanny pack and tosses it to me. Oh, the fanny pack! How she ever made fun of Bert for his "man purse" is beyond me.

I unfold the paper as slowly as possible, mostly to annoy her. That's what best friends do.

I've never seen more cursive or exclamation points on a page in my life. It takes my eyes a second to adjust, like those folders with the holograms on them that you have to tilt one way and then another to see the image. But when I do see it, I wish I could immediately go back to *un*seeing it.

I drop the paper like it might detonate. "Oh no. No, no, no, no, no."

"I'm not asking you to do it! Just help me with it!" Coralee grabs my hand. "Puh-leeeeease!"

Before I can say no again, a remote control truck with very bright headlights and a not-so-quiet siren zooms into my room, followed by two not-so-quiet boys.

"Give it to me!" Patrick yells.

"It's been five minutes! Mom said it was my turn!" Finn screams, and jumps onto my bed as Patrick makes a grab for him.

"Boys," Meg calls from down the hall. "Get out of your sister's room!"

Finn holds the remote as high as he can. Patrick head-butts him in the stomach. Finn bursts into tears, and they both fall into a tangle on the bed. The truck bumps me repeatedly in the knee like it doesn't know who these people are and could I please adopt it?

Meg comes in, grabs the remote and the truck and the boys, and backs out again with an apology in my general direction.

My blue comforter is now covered in small dirty footprints. Coralee raises an eyebrow and flicks the paper a centimeter closer to me.

I read the cursive lettering at the top. And then I read it one more time for good measure. *The Oklahoma Little Miss Boots and Bows Pageant wants YOU!* I shiver. Why so aggressive?

It sounds like an army recruitment poster. Or a cult. To be honest, either of those options seems better than sitting here for the next month getting run over by toy trucks and patronized by my dad. Maybe that's how they get people—*Come to us, all you who are lonely! Whose parents have abandoned you! Who need to kill time and escape your own thoughts!* But a beauty pageant? Really?

A sneaky flash of interest must flit across my face, though, and Coralee snaps it up like a dog with a scrap of meat. Gone before I can take it back. She claps her hands and shouts, "Let the pageant season begin!"

Great. One moment of weakness and now I'm going to have to find a reason to back out of something I never even said yes to.

I don't believe in telepathy. But just in case, I yell in my head as loud as I can, *Mom, wherever you are right now, I want you to know this is all your fault!*

5

Smooth Sailing

"Shall I record the minutes?" Bert asks, flipping his laptop open on his knees. In the dimness of the canning shed, his face glows blue from the light.

Why are we hiding in the canning shed next to the garage beside the carport instead of in the nice air-conditioned trailer? Because it's the only safe place to escape from little eyes and ears and also bigger eyes and ears. I thought the boys were bad. But Dad is *everywhere*—when I'm rolling down the rows of the garden with a basket in my lap, trying to gather the ripest tomatoes for BLTs, when I'm in the kitchen frying up the bacon for said BLTs, when I'm attempting to get the boys to sit still long enough to work on their outer space puzzle, when I'm tossing a load of laundry in the dryer after Meg used up the last of the towels without realizing it. It's been less than forty-eight hours since Mom and Hutch left, and if there's a square inch next to me, he's there!

To be fair, there's not a whole lot of "there" to go. The trailer might be outfitted now for all my wheelchair needs, but it is still about the size of two living rooms slapped together. You can park yourself in the middle of the laundry room, reach out your hands, and touch both walls. Without work to distract him, I think Dad's getting stir-crazy. The canning shed seems to be my only safe space.

Coralee shifts next to me, her purple leggings sticking to the cement blocks that line the walls and floor. This place used to be covered in shelves filled with mason jars of okra and beans and tomatoes and peaches and anything else Mema could can from her garden. Since she moved out, Hutch and I turned it into a makeshift workout room. I've got my stretchy bands, weights, and a yoga ball in here. The smell of dirt drifting in from outside soothes me. Coralee tugs at her tights again. I smile. Bonus of a wheelchair? You always have a comfortable place to sit.

"No one needs the minutes, dude," Coralee says to Bert.

"You don't know what you need. That's why I'm here," he says while he's tap-tapping away.

"I agreed to *allow* you to be our manager because you said one of your brothers or sisters could drive us to the pageant location if Susie can't do it," Coralee explains.

I lean over to watch him type—*Susie can't do it.*

"And I agreed to help you because history has proven that you are a disorganized person who tends to . . ." Bert trails off, searching for the right word.

"Fly by the seat of your pants," I offer.

Bert nods. "Yes, exactly."

"Untrue!" she shouts.

"When you did the pageant in Checotah last summer—" he starts, and she narrows her eyes. "You didn't bring a backup player for your song. So when the sound system glitched, you had to sing along with your phone. Do you have any idea how bad the sound quality is on that generation Samsung?"

"Do you have any idea how easy it would be to break every one of your fingers so you could never type again?" Coralee asks sweetly.

I grab one of the stretchy bands and whip it at Coralee. "We are way ahead of ourselves here. I haven't officially agreed to help because you haven't officially told me a single thing about this pageant and why, out of all the pageants that have come before, this one is *the most important thing in the universe.*"

Coralee stands, her body silhouetted by the light pouring in from the driveway. Behind her, heat rises from the pavement in aggressive waves. It's June in Oklahoma. Everything that isn't aggressive is dead.

"Four reasons." She holds up three fingers. Bert perks up, his hands twitching over the keys of his laptop.

"One," she says, "the Little Miss Boots and Bows Pageant is HUGE. There's one in every state, and if you win in Oklahoma, you get to compete in the nationals with all the other Little Miss Boots and Bows."

I giggle. How could I not? Coralee doesn't even pause to threaten me. Her eyes are glazed with pageant fever.

"Two, this is the first time it's ever been close enough for me to enter. It's in Henryetta this year. Less than forty miles! It's in the Rocking Horse Theater."

Bert stops typing. "Interesting."

I look between the two of them. "What? What's interesting?"

He turns to me. "The Rocking Horse Theater is an Oklahoma landmark. All the seats rock. It only shows black-and-white films. Its slogan is 'Rock away your cares and revisit the good old days at the Rocking Horse.'"

I glance at Coralee. "Why is that interesting?" She shrugs. We stare Bert down until he explains.

He turns to Coralee. "It appears to me that your Boots and Bows pageant is on its way out."

"What does *that* mean?" Coralee asks.

"I think the current generation of young adults would rather not be assigned a pronoun, much less a title like 'Little Miss.' Also, the fact that it is held this year in a theater that prioritizes tradition over current trends suggests that this pageant is running out of both monetary and societal support."

Coralee reaches over and flicks his laptop shut. Then she takes both his hands in hers, and the look on her face can only be described as *imminent total destruction*. It's too late for me and Bert, but if Finn and Patrick were here, I'd tell them to run for cover.

"Bert. Listen to me. I want this pageant. I want to be crowned Oklahoma's Little Miss Boots and Bows more than I've ever wanted anything in my whole entire life. And if you so much as utter one more word against it, I *will* end you. Do you understand?"

Bert nods, but he doesn't look scared. He's the only person besides me that Coralee can't intimidate.

"I support you," he says. "Of course I do. My feelings on the pageant are irrelevant. You're my friend, and I will help in any way I can."

She looks surprised and then a little teary before she

squeezes his hands once and lets go. Bert's also the only person who can bring Coralee back from the edge.

"Reason number three," she says now. "The registration fee is seventy-five dollars, and I just so happen to have seventy-six dollars and four cents saved up from my Girl Scout cookie sales this spring."

"You aren't in the Girl Scouts," I point out.

"Doesn't mean I can't sell 'em. I *may* have borrowed a few dozen boxes from the stand outside Food & Co. while Sierra and her pals were on a bathroom break."

"You stole cookies in front of my father's grocery store?" Bert asks. I bet he's regretting his promise of unconditional support *now*.

"And from Sierra, who is in our class?" I add.

"And who also competes in pageants, so all's fair in love and war," Coralee shoots back. "*Plus*, she's spending this summer in Oklahoma City doing some artsy-fartsy thing at the OKC Museum of Art, so she's out of the running."

Wow. Art camp. That's actually pretty cool. Ever since Sierra asked for the recipe for the snowball cookies I made in speech class in sixth grade, we've been on a truce. I would never tell Coralee this, but Sierra's not half bad as humans go.

"Oh, and fourth," Coralee adds, almost like it's an

afterthought, "my mom has to report to court for a speed-ing ticket in Henryetta at the end of June, so she'll be there on the final day of the pageant." She looks away as Bert types. "Maybe she'll have time to drop by."

Ever since I've known Coralee, her mom has been trying to "get herself together." That's why Coralee lives next door with her grandpa Dane and his wife, Susie, and their trailer full of cockatoos and a pit bull named Daisy. I've only met her mom once. Coralee looks just like her. Big blue eyes. Bigger blond hair. And loud. Except unlike Coralee, she never sticks around long enough to finish a sentence. But Coralee adores her. She'd never admit it, but I know she does these pageants for her. Her mom was Miss Southeast Tulsa back in her day.

I watch Coralee, twisting her shirt up in a knot and humming an old country song I only recognize because of her. I vow right here and now to help her win this pageant.

"Well," I say, "minus the fact that my mom will never sign off on me riding with one of your siblings to the rock-ing whatever—"

"The Rocking Horse," Bert and Coralee chime in unison.

"And the fact that I have never once been to a beauty pageant and will be no help, or even maybe negative help, if that's possible—" Coralee is already dancing in place before I get to my big finish. "I'm in." *Please don't let this be a cult. Please don't let this be a cult.*

"*Yeah*, you are!" she says, and slaps me with my own stretchy band. Then she slaps Bert, too, who says, "Watch the device," and hugs his computer to him.

"Now all we have to do is practice for the interview, pick the world's most perfect song for the talent portion, and find a formal dress for free, because I am out of money!" She cheers.

Oh good. Smooth sailing from here.

6

Wiglets and Your Sunday Best

Dear Mom,

It is Day Six of my confinement. I have begun to carve notches in my bedpost to mark the days.

The alien visitors to this planet seem to be mostly harmless, though the small ones appear more destructive than their larger counterparts.

If you receive this note, then I have been swallowed in a pit of LEGOs and my father's good intentions.

JK. Having a good time here. Meg took me into town to buy more baking supplies

at Food & Co. and LEGOs for the boys. Bert's
dad said to tell you congrats again on getting hitched to Hutch.

Hope you're having fun on Route 66. Kiss
the pavement for me when you hit Miami,
Oklahoma, and make sure you say it right—
My-AM-uh—or they'll send you packing.

Peace,

El

I read over the email one more time, making sure
it's peppy enough so she won't turn the RV around and
show up on the doorstep. No need to mention the crayon
drawings of every scene from *How to Train Your Dragon*
that the boys drew on my shower door. Or the Matilda
Jane matching shirt and skort Meg purchased because she
thought they would look *just adorable* on me. Or the fact
that Dad has started taking more calls from the law firm
despite his "sabbatical." Fine by me if he wants to work his
way through the vacation. Why does he think there are
two peach pies, a loaf of brioche, and three dozen thumbprint cookies on the kitchen counter? The busier we both
are, the better.

I miss Mema. She'd take one look at this situation, slap
her hands on her knees, stand up from the rocking couch,

and get to work putting us all in our places. *Ellie, snap beans for supper. Greg, you help her. Boys, here's a sponge and some Comet. I want to see that shower door sparkle. Meg, no more ruffles. Ellie hates ruffles. Done and done.* But Mema doesn't drive much anymore, and she's got her hands full with Grandpa. Also, between her gardening club and quilting club and the checkers tournaments, which she has been disqualified from three times for cheating, her social calendar is full. I tap my fingers on the windowsill and stare out at the gravel road. Wish I could say the same.

And then I see the dust cloud coming and race down the hallway like it's the roller derby. I'm halfway out the front door before Susie's maroon Cadillac crawls into the drive.

"Dad, I'm running errands with Coralee and Bert!" I shout. I don't even know where he is, but the house isn't big enough for anyone to be out of earshot, *ever*.

I'm shutting the door when his hand snakes out to stop it. He's armed with a cup of coffee and his laptop. Ready for Vacation Workday Number Six.

"Wait, Ellie." He looks from me to Susie, who's hanging her arm out the driver's-side window with an unlit cigarette dangling from her fingers. "Where are you going?"

It takes everything in me not to ignore him and roll away.

"To run errands," I repeat. Errands—the adult answer for everything because it is both vague and also important-sounding.

He leans forward, trying to see past the glare on the windshield. "With who, now?" Susie waves, her arm jiggling merrily. Coralee leans over from the passenger seat and toots the horn.

"Susie, Coralee's grandpa's wife, and Coralee, and Bert, Mr. Akers the grocer's son." Dad looks at me like that was clear as mud, but it's not my job to draw him a family tree. He can learn like the rest of us, by putting in the time. And I don't owe him an explanation for any of this. He might be my dad by blood, but that doesn't mean he gets to parent me.

He opens his mouth. "See ya," I say before he can ask another question. Then I am rolling into the sun and over to Bert, who waits by the open door, ready to fold my wheelchair and stick it in the trunk after I transfer myself to the back seat. I don't usually get nervous with a transfer, but with Dad watching, my hands get sweaty on the brakes, and it takes two tries for me to push with my arms before I can slide myself over. I don't look back to see if he noticed. Because the worst thing in the world wouldn't be catching him with a disappointed look on his face. It would be seeing that he didn't even wait to watch.

"You kids ready for an adventure?" Susie asks once

we're cruising down Route 9. She flicks her unlit cigarette onto the dash and fluffs her frosted bangs in the rearview mirror. "Lord help me, I miss my smokes."

I point to the pack tucked into the cupholder by her elbow. "What about those?"

She pats them without looking. "These here are for moral support." Then she lifts the sleeve of her floral shirt-dress to show three round bandages. "I'm quittin'. Got my nicotine patches and my nicotine gum. But sometimes I just like to hold one for comfort."

I watch the unlit cigarette slide around on the dash.

"She went from two packs of Camels a day to two packs of Nicorette a day, but I'm trying to get her to start up again," Coralee says with a wicked grin, her hair blowing wild in the wind as she turns toward us. "She was a whole lot nicer when she smoked."

Susie swats her arm. "Hush now, or I'll turn this baby around and there'll be no Little Miss anything for you."

Coralee pops her Bubblicious and gives Susie her best pageant smile. It's a little terrifying, like those creepy Annalee dolls Mema used to put up around the trailer for Christmas until Grandpa hid them in the garage behind his electric saw. "I will be on my best behavior. I swear." She crosses her heart with one hand and crosses her fingers behind her back with the other.

"Could you roll that up, please?" Bert asks next to me as a handful of papers flap around in his arms, blown by the wind pouring in his open window.

"Sorry, Berto. AC's on the fritz," Coralee yells. Susie hits the automatic buttons on her door. All four windows go up, and a cool draft from the vents begins to blow.

"She's just messin' with you, son. Air works just fine," Susie says.

Coralee huffs and slides a pair of red rhinestone sunglasses down over her nose. "Suit yourself. But every good adventure starts with the windows down."

Bert smooths his hair and then tries to do the same for the papers on his lap. It's a major fail on both accounts, but I ask, "Why don't you tell us what you got there?" before he starts to worry over it again.

He holds up the first slightly crumpled sheet and clears his throat. "Rules and Regulations," he announces, and Coralee lifts her big camera to take a pic. Bert startles.

I point at the camera. "Um, why?"

"All in good time, Ellie Cowan. Win first. Ask questions later." She winks. I make a grab for the camera, but she holds it out of reach.

"Tell me or I quit before we even get started," I demand.

"*Fine.* If you must know, I am documenting all the precious moments in the making so we can cherish these photos forever," she says. "Also, when I become famous, Hollywood's going to need some old footage of me for their documentary."

I order my face to freeze. It's the only way to hold in the laughter.

"I got some of them scissors back home that cut wavy lines, if you want to do some scrapbooking," Susie offers. Coralee's sunglasses might be dark, but they aren't dark enough to hide that eye roll.

"As I was saying," Bert continues, ignoring all of us, "the Rules and Regulations state that this is an all-natural system."

"What does *that* mean?" I ask.

He scans the sheet. "No hairpieces, wigs, wiglets, padding, or makeup on children under four."

"This pageant allows kids as little as four?"

"Actually," Bert says to me, "it goes all the way down to Under Ones."

"Well, that gives me all the bad vibes." I shiver. "And *what* is a wiglet?"

"The child of a full-grown wig?" Coralee giggles.

"And what do they mean by padding?" I add.

"I'm not certain I want to know." Bert clears his throat, looking deeply uncomfortable. "However, I do know that casual wear may be bought off-the-rack or custom-made.

And formal wear should be considered as Sunday best, Easter dress, party dress, flower girl, or junior prom–style."

"If someone shows up in a flower-girl dress, I am not responsible for what I might say or do," Coralee announces.

"No guardians allowed onstage for children five and up," Bert continues.

"You hear that, Susie? Try as you might, you can't come up there with the Aqua Net and eyeshadow."

Susie puts a hand to her chest and heaves a big, dramatic sigh. "Break my heart, why don'tcha?"

Bert turns to his second pages of notes. "Scoring: judges are qualified professionals from different industries."

"That means car salesmen and former Little Misses," Coralee explains.

"The interview takes place during casual wear, and contestants are judged on character, personality, stage presence, and overall modeling of their outfit, not the outfit itself."

"Yeah right, not the outfit," Coralee scoffs. "Last year in Checotah, a girl literally gave the answer to world peace and they tanked her because she wore a scrunchy in her hair."

Bert holds up a hand like he's a witness about to take the stand. "I am only here to share the rules. Let's hope the Little Miss Boots and Bows judges are more open-minded."

"Bert, did you even hear yourself just now?" I ask.

He sighs. "I did. Let's continue. During formal wear, contestants are judged on facial beauty, poise, self-confidence, and presentation."

Ick. The whole thing makes me squirm, like I've just come out of a public restroom and despite washing my hands a zillion times, I *for sure* have microscopic bits of someone else's pee on me. But up front, Coralee nods and pumps her fist on the cracked leather seat. She wants this. And if she wants it, I'm going to pretend not to be nauseated by the whole thing, and help her get it.

7

The More the Merrier

The Rocking Horse Theater sits in the center of Henryetta in a strip of one-story redbrick buildings lined up together like dominoes. We pass by a dry cleaner's, a florist, a drugstore with boarded-up windows, and a tractor supply shop before catching sight of the theater's marquee.

As Susie curses and attempts to parallel park along the street, I lean out my window to read the black letters stuck on the bright white sign above the glass-and-gold front doors. In big letters at the top it reads: PLAYING NOW: HIS GIRL FRIDAY. And then underneath, in much smaller letters, it reads: WELCOME, OKLAHOMA'S LITTLE MISS BOOTS AND BOWS CONTESTANTS! The *S* in "Bows" has come loose and sags below the rest like an undone shoelace.

When Susie finally manages to wrestle the Caddy into place, Bert hops out first to get my chair. Coralee stands with her hands on her hips and her back to me, studying the sign and the tarnished gold around the front door, which is propped open with a brick. Whatever glory this place once held has clearly faded. But when Coralee turns to me after I'm in my chair, she is all smiles. She doesn't see the fingerprint smudges on the ticket booth window or the trash piled up in the alley or even the rusted mechanical horse out front that has a handwritten OUT OF ORDER sign taped over the coin slot. She's seeing this as her ticket out of here—her shot to stardom and to proving to her mom once and for all that she's a somebody. I wish I had her talent—not the triple-threat kind but the ability to see a situation for all its promises instead of its pitfalls. I blame Dad's genes for that one. The only time I can turn it off is when I'm baking. When I'm in the kitchen, I'm golden. I wish I were there now.

Susie waves at us from the car, where she pulls out a magazine and fishes her unlit cigarette off the dashboard.

"You ready to rock this thing?" I ask in my pump-it-up voice as we approach the glass doors like Dorothy and her cohorts walking into Oz.

"Ready to rock and roll, Els," she says, and hip-checks my shoulder.

"Technically, all we're doing is turning in your registration form and fees. There is no actual competition today," Bert informs us.

Coralee pops her gum and hip-checks him, too. "Don't burst my bubble, Bert."

With a deep breath I know she doesn't want us to see, Coralee steps into the cool, dim air of the Rocking Horse Theater and we follow.

"The posters said this way, right?" I ask as I roll over stale kernels of old popcorn in front of the concession stand and down the hallway, where the water fountain leaks a damp puddle on the paisley carpet. Just past the bathrooms, which smell suspiciously and overwhelmingly like Febreze, two red velvet ropes stretch out to form an aisle leading into the one and only theater. A poster-board sign propped up next to the entrance reads, REGISTRATION FOR THE LITTLE MISS BOOTS AND BOWS PAGEANT FROM 12 P.M. TO 4 P.M. CASH OR CHECK ONLY. NO REFUNDS. PLEASE READ AND SIGN ALL MATERIALS BEFORE ENTERING. KEEP THE LINE MOVING. EXIT BACK RIGHT OF THE AUDITORIUM IMMEDIATELY ONCE REGISTRATION HAS BEEN PROCESSED.

Somebody very serious and very into their schedule

made that sign. I bet they own an Apple Watch *and* a day planner. Bert will be right at home.

Inside the Rocking Horse auditorium, it looks pretty much like any other theater. I could be back in Nashville at the Regal. Except in front of the rows of brown-and-orange theater seats, there are also tables and rocking chairs like somebody's about to order lunch at Cracker Barrel. The theater seats do not have handicapped rows with spaces left at the ends. If someone in a wheelchair wanted to attend a show, they better be ready to sit up front and center at one of those tables. Good thing I don't care for black-and-white movies.

Coralee marches down the aisle and takes her place by the stage, where a folding table is set up for people to check in by last name. I am more than happy to let her take the lead. Bert sits at one of the round theater tables, and I pull up next to him. He retrieves his laptop from his satchel, scans the room, and begins to write.

"What are you doing?"

"Taking notes on the competition," he says without looking up at me.

There aren't that many people here. Over by the stage, two moms have spread blankets on the grubby carpet to let their babies roll around. Babies in tiaras. That's a scary thought. A handful of girls who look to be about our age sit at another table with their heads close together. They are all white and blond and . . . shiny. No surprise there. One Black girl sits by herself in the first row of seats, hair curtaining her face, which is bent over a book. Her arms curl protectively around it like it's a secret, which of course makes me want to ask her what she's reading. And that's the entire sum and total of the Little Miss Boots and Bows crowd. Maybe we're early? Or late? Or better yet, let's hope this is it and Coralee will sweep the competition.

I'm about to point this out to Bert when Coralee runs up to us, breathless. "I need a pen! I forgot to sign my name on the photo waiver!"

"This is what I mean about being prepared."

She dances in place, impatient. "Not *now*, Bert."

He holds out his favorite Bic and she snatches it up, but before she can race off to the table again, a woman with black hair shellacked in a tight bob walks up to us. She is tiny, as in just a smidge above my eye level tiny. Her blazer and skirt are white with cherry-red stripes to match her lipstick and heels, which look two sizes too big below her birdlike ankles. When she cups her hands together in front of her as if in prayer and smiles, my skin prickles. There's something sharp there. A smile with a bite.

"Well, who do we have here?" she asks in the raspy

voice of a chronic smoker. We should offer her some of Susie's gum.

Coralee turns around so fast her hair whips me in the face.

"Mrs. Perkins, hi. I found a pen!" Wow. Nervous Coralee. That right there was worth the forty-minute drive.

"Please, dear, I might be in charge of this show, but you can call me Rae Ann," she says. But she's not looking at Coralee. She is staring directly at me with laser focus. This lady runs a pageant? She could use some manners. "Please, introduce me to your friends." It's not a question.

"Oh, right, yeah. This is Bert and that's Ellie." Coralee waves back at us without a glance.

Bert, who is typing at lightning speed, tilts his head briefly toward her, as if he is tipping a cap. He's probably typing notes about her. I want to read over his shoulder.

Rae Ann bends down, and I catch a whiff of sickly sweet rose perfume, like a cheap car freshener. I lean back slightly.

"Ellie, it is *so* nice to meet you. I can take your registration form up to the table for you if you like?" There's that smile again.

"Yeah, no. I'm not entering. I'm just here with Coralee."

She crosses her arms and purses her lips. "Oh, really? What a shame. You have a face for the stage, darlin'!"

How about the rest of me? I want to ask, since she is carefully avoiding looking at my chair, but I don't say anything because Coralee is nodding furiously behind her. I shake my head no at her. She nods yes back. We are in a head-bobbing battle of the wills, when Coralee cheats.

"She'd love to!" she says, and Rae Ann claps her hands.

"She doesn't have the seventy-five-dollar registration fee," Bert, my beautiful, beautiful friend, points out.

"He's right! I don't! And the rules are very specific," I say, but Rae Ann is already waving away our logic.

"Don't worry about that, sweetheart. You can drop it off at rehearsals. Now, why don't we get you up to the table to get that form!" And then, before I can say a word, her cherry-red nails are on the back of my purple-striped chair, my *chair* that is just as much a part of me as my arm or my leg. She is pushing me toward the sign-up table.

I grab the wheels. We jerk to a stop. "No one touches my chair without my permission."

A second passes where this could go one of two ways: Rae Ann apologizes and learns a valuable life lesson or . . . "Well, sure, dear. I was just helping you along," she says without so much as a wince over what she has just done.

"How about I go fetch it and bring it back to you so you don't tire yourself out?"

I watch her walk away, her tiny steps in that tight skirt making their way toward my doom. I spin around to Coralee. She is dancing in place and nodding yes. "I'm sorry, do you have to go to the bathroom?" I ask. "Because that must be the reason you are looking so antsy about something."

"Pleasepleasepleasepleaseplease," she begs.

"No."

She gets down on her knees on the sticky floor and clasps her hands together. "PLEASE."

"NO."

"Here you go, sweetheart," Rae Ann says, waving a form in front of my face and successfully ending the standoff.

I give her a blank stare. "I don't have a pen."

Coralee tosses the Bic to me, and I catch it without looking, because I have stupid awesome reflexes. "Here you go!" she says cheerily. If I punch her, would that be enough to disqualify me?

I look back at Bert, who is watching us over the edge of his laptop. Behind him, the girl in the seats has put her book down to take in the show. Heat starts to creep up my neck until I feel it in my cheeks. Never have I ever wanted to be center stage of this kind of attention, and I don't plan to start now.

"Fine," I mutter so people will stop staring, and roll back over to the table to write, but not because I plan to do one single thing in this pageant. I put pen to paper, and Coralee snaps a photo. I will fill out this form. No one says I have to show up.

8

You Scream, I Scream, We All Scream

Francis the cockatoo raises his head, hops up onto my knee, and opens his black beak wide. When I got home from the Rocking Horse Horror Show, I angry-chopped a boatload of fruit and turned it into Nadiya Hussain's fruit salad fattoush. I can't watch *The Great British Baking Show* now that Mary Berry's gone. I'm exclusively a *Nadiya Bakes* girl now. She was my favorite in the original anyway.

I'm over at Coralee's now, and the birds are going crazy over the tortilla strips dipped in cinnamon and sugar. I hold up another toasted bit of tortilla, and Francis delicately snatches it out of my hand. I wish everyone in the trailer were as gentle. Coralee lies on the floor of her bedroom, hurling a tennis ball at the wall, which Daisy the pit bull occasionally intercepts. There's a lot of hostility and slobber swirling around this room.

"I cannot believe you won't do it."

"I can't believe you ever thought I would!"

"But you filled out the form!" she argues.

"Because everyone was staring at me and Rae Ann freaks me out!"

Coralee lobs the ball down the hallway. Daisy launches herself after it like a rocket, and Coralee slams the door. "Rae Ann Perkins is the pageant coordinator and also Little Miss Boots and Bows 1986. She is a queen and my idol."

"But she's not mine."

"Do it for meeeeee." Coralee crawls up onto the bed, shooing Francis, who nips at her tank top and sidles along the headboard until he is directly over me.

I point a finger up at him. "Don't even think about pooping on me or no more fattoush for you."

"He won't. Didn't I tell you? Dane's got them all potty trained now. We keep a litter box in the laundry room."

"No kidding?" I imagine Francis and his friends huddled around a cat box like it's the port-a-potty at the campgrounds.

"Don't change the subject. I need you to do this."

"But why?" I ask her. "You've done this before perfectly fine on your own. You don't need me to help you win."

"Maybe I do!" She throws herself back on the bed, her feet by my face and her face by my feet like we lie during sleepovers. "I've never even placed before," she says to the ceiling.

"You never told me that."

"Well, it's embarrassing."

"No, it's not. Everything takes practice."

"You won third this year and first last year at the bake-off at church," she points out.

I want to tell her I'm still mad my French silk pie with the cinnamon whipped cream placed third. But now isn't the time.

Coralee flicks my toe. "Maybe I need you there to push me harder? Having someone else in it who I can trade off interview questions with and test my vocals on could be a game changer. Plus"—she sits up—"it'll be fun."

Interviews and fancy dresses in front of a theater full of spectators. *Fun.* I love Coralee. I do. But I can't get the look on Rae Ann's face out of my head—hungry and pitying at the same time—like I'm the dog with the weepy eyes in the Humane Society commercials. She wants to rescue me to feel good about herself.

I grab Coralee's hand and squeeze. "I'm sorry, but I can't."

Dad does not ask about my "errands" when I get home. But he does ask how I like my fish. He's wearing Mema's frilly blue apron that says KISS THE COOK in cursive. Maybe he feels guilty for all the work calls. Maybe he actually missed me today while I was gone. Or maybe he just really likes fish.

We assemble under the carport to watch him scrape the fish off the grill and onto a plate. He loses half of it in the coals. But the pieces he manages to catch look okay enough to me until he drowns them in a pool of garlic-butter sauce that has already begun to separate—tiny spots of oil rise to the surface like tadpoles.

Once the fish is unloaded, we decide to eat outside on the porch under the bug zapper despite the heat. Everyone gathers around the low table in front of the rocking couch.

"Okay," Meg says, sweeping her curls, damp from sweat, off the back of her neck and then stretching out her arms. "Everybody take a hand."

Finn grabs my right hand and Dad reaches out palm up until I put my left hand in his. They all bow heads. Well, this is new. Then, to get even weirder, they all say, in unison, "Father, we thank you for this family dinner. Amen," the boys dragging out the *A* in "Amen" so it has eleven syllables and hits four octaves. I close my eyes just as they are opening theirs to hide my surprise. They have a group prayer? We haven't said it since they've been here. Why now? If this is their way to ease me into it, it didn't work. My stomach flops over, but not from hunger. Must be nice. Must be just peachy to be able to say "family" like it's a solid unit instead of the choppy aloneness of "Mom and me."

I drop Dad's hand first and pick up my fork. I take a bite of pearly white fish to have something to do that doesn't involve talking.

"How is it?" Dad asks, his eyebrows peaked with worry. So much for avoiding conversation.

I take a minute. The fish is sweet underneath all the butter and garlic. Not bad, really. But there's also something bitter that I can't place, and I definitely shouldn't have to work this hard to chew it. It's seafood, not gum.

"Does the chef approve?" He forgot to take off the blue apron. It bunches around his neck like an old lady's scarf as he hunches forward to watch me try to swallow.

I manage to nod, still grinding my teeth over the grainy bits.

"This is your dad's famous grilled sea bass." Meg beams.

"He created the marinade himself. I swear he makes this at least once a week in the summer."

"At *least*," Patrick adds, avoiding the fish and shoveling fries into his mouth like he's afraid his mom will take them hostage at any moment.

Finn spits fish flesh across the table. "This one tastes different."

"That's ridiculous." Dad holds up a tiny sliver of fish on his fork for inspection. We all pause to watch. He sniffs. He gingerly places it on his tongue. And then he lets it sit there for ages like a communion wafer before swallowing. The look on his face is enough to make my own mouth go dry. I spit the last little bits into my napkin while he's not looking.

"I don't get it," he mumbles, turning the fish over with his knife to check the bottom. "I bought it yesterday from Food & Co. It was on display in the green cooler right next to the seafood case. It should be fine."

Oh *no*.

I throw my hands out toward Finn and Patrick like I'm trying to stop them from hurtling into traffic. "Did it have a sticker on it? A *green* sticker?"

Dad nods.

"Drop your forks!" They do. "Green sticker foods are markdowns. They are *take-and-make*."

Dad cocks his head at me like he doesn't understand. Of course he doesn't. He hasn't been here long enough to know the rules.

"Take-and-make," I say again for emphasis, "means take and make *immediately*. It's discounted because it's hours away from the trash can. This fish is one day past its *last* day." Dad stares at me. He still doesn't get it. "So, you know, basically poisonous."

Both Finn and Patrick shove back from the table and dance around the porch making gagging sounds and wiping their tongues with napkins. Meg very slowly brings a hand up to her throat. Dad already looks a little green, but I think that's from embarrassment rather than actual food poisoning. I scour the roof of my mouth with my tongue, searching for bits of take-and-make. I don't think any of us ate enough to get sick, but it's clear this meal is a disaster.

I take a *huge* gulp of ice water, then clap my hands so everybody turns. "Who's up for ice cream for dinner?" The boys cheer. Meg looks like she could kiss me, even though I'm not the one wearing the apron, and Dad? Dad looks like he ate a hot coal from the grill and would like to suck on it a while. As I roll back from the table, I half expect smoke to start pouring from his ears.

The rocking couch is packed with four bodies, and not

for the first time am I grateful for the separate space of my chair as we all hold bowls filled to the brim with chocolate-covered-cherry ice cream with bits of my thumbprint cookies crumbled on top.

Dad closes his eyes after the first bite and sighs. I smile into my bowl. The sugar seems to have a calming effect. That and hauling the fish in a giant Hefty bag all the way to the metal trash cans under the carport. Out of sight, out of mind. That's how Dad works. I guess that's how he avoided missing me all these years. My smile slips but nobody notices. Good food can do that—smooth over all the moods.

"Ellie," Finn says, his eyes bright and hair extra fluffy from the humidity. "You're my hero."

"Thanks, kid," I say, and catch Dad nodding in agreement out of the corner of my eye.

I would never say this to his face, but it's kind of awesome to watch my all-capable, ever-ready dad royally mess up. Maybe this whole living-together thing won't be so bad. Maybe we can really do this now. I'm not asking for a father-daughter montage of perfect moments. But less awkwardness so I can survive this month would be nice.

After the sun sinks behind the trees and the fireflies begin to blink in between the garden rows, Meg ushers the boys inside. Dad and I sit in silence for a while and it's okay . . . until I open my mouth.

"So, ummm, you'll never believe what happened today."

"Yeah?" Dad smiles with his hands on his stomach, like a satisfied Santa.

"I got asked to be in a beauty pageant." I throw him a grin, expecting him to grin back so we can laugh about the whole thing together. But he stops rocking on the couch and sits up.

"You what?"

I shift in my seat. Why do I feel like I just landed in the principal's office? "Uh, yeah. Coralee is entering the Little Miss Boots and Bows Pageant, and me and Bert went with her to the sign-ups, and they asked me to join."

Dad leans forward, elbows on his knees. "Did they ask for a credit card? Is it some kind of scam?" His eyes dart from my face to my chair so fast I would have thought I'd imagined it if I didn't know him better. Something that just minutes ago began to lighten inside me like daybreak crashes down into darkness again.

He thinks there's no way they would want someone like me, a girl with cerebral palsy in a wheelchair, to be in their fancy pageant. Of *course*. He might eat the ice cream, but he still thinks I'm pathetic.

"No, *Dad*, it seems legit. It's been around for, like, a hundred years." Why does he automatically have to assume it's a trick just because they asked *me*? "But I'm not doing it." When I said that to Coralee I felt strong, but now, saying it to Dad, I feel weak and small.

He sits backs, blinks a couple of times, and shakes his head like he's waking up.

"Well, that's good to know." He laughs once, more like a cough. I force myself to laugh back and then make an excuse about being tired and go inside.

I grab a Ping-Pong ball from the jar on the table next to my bed and crawl down into the sewing-machine corner. Number seven: *Wiggle your toes, wiggle your fingers, wiggle your eyebrows. SMILE.* I throw the ball across the room, where it bounces off the wall with a harmless plink. Not tonight. Not a chance.

He doesn't think I can do it because of the wheelchair. He thinks I can't handle it. He's too busy feeling *sorry* for me to even imagine the possibility that I might win.

I kick the wall with my heel. It's just like that one time at swim therapy.

Once when I was six, Mom had parent-teacher conferences at the school where she taught, so Dad had to take me to swim therapy instead of her. It was at the clinic with my favorite therapist, Kaska. We had the small indoor pool all to ourselves. Parents weren't allowed inside the pool area, so Dad sat outside and watched through the round porthole window. When Mom took me, she would hold up notes after each lap that said things like, *Go Flipper!* and *Keep calm and swim on!* Dad didn't hold up notes, but I didn't care. I was just glad he came.

I swam my hardest that day, scissor-kicking my legs like Kaska told me and pointing my toes, even though my calves ached and my neck hurt from holding my head above water.

When I wheeled out, wrapped in a towel and still in my swimsuit because I was too embarrassed to ask Dad to help me change, he burst into applause, and I thought I would die from happiness.

"Ellie, my girl! You were fantastic!" he crowed. "Do you know what I heard a little boy tell his mom when he walked by and saw you?" I shook my head, bubbles of joy bursting in my chest. "He said he couldn't even tell you needed therapy. You swam just like a regular kid!"

The joy fizzled out like a used-up sparkler. He wasn't proud. He was *surprised*—that I finally did something "regular." What's so special about being regular?

I pick up my phone, hit Coralee's name, and shoot her a text message.

Three words: Let's do this.

9

Share the Love

"That is not how you smile." Bert peers over his clip-board. He's positioned himself pretty nicely under an umbrella and a straw hat, with shades low on his sunscreen-slathered nose, and a Yeti mug full of lemonade by his side. He's having a mighty fine day at the beach. I cannot say the same.

"It *is* how I smile. I don't have another smile," I argue from my spot in the blazing sun. The water slaps the shore behind me. It's the lake calling out, *Ellie, the water's just fine. Why don't you come in, take a load off?* Why don't I? Oh yeah, in the heat of a very bad moment, I agreed to enter the Little Miss Boots and Bows Pageant, and I have spent the last four days regretting it.

Bert takes a sip of his lemonade. "Smile like you didn't just bite your tongue."

"Say *cheeeeeese!*" Coralee singsongs, and catches me mid-grimace. She looks down at the screen of her digital camera and frowns. "He's right. That is not a good look on you. Did you actually taste blood on that one?"

"That's it, I quit." I take two big breaths before muscling my chair out of the sand and into the shade under Bert's umbrella—it is rainbow-striped with tassels. I dig in his satchel, slung across the back of his chair, for some ChapStick.

"Don't get sand in there."

"Just because you're the manager doesn't mean you get to boss me around about everything." I flick a little sand in his lap. He sighs like an old man and then spends several minutes brushing it off.

Coralee plops down in front of us in her bright pink bikini. It says "Beach Bum" in glitter on her backside. "Let's take a break anyway. We need to talk about the rehearsal this Saturday."

"Excuse me, the what?"

"*Rehearsal,*" Bert and Coralee say in unison.

"What do we need to rehearse? We show up in two and a half weeks, answer questions in our casual wear, show off our extraordinary talents, and then prance around again

73

in very uncomfortable *fancy dress*, no wiglets allowed."

Coralee kicks sand on me. Bert huffs and shakes the debris off his foot.

"No, dummy. Rehearsal for the performance of the Little Miss Boots and Bows song."

I slide my sunglasses up onto my forehead to better see her face. Because surely she is kidding. This is a Coralee joke—like the time she told me we were playing musical chairs in gym class. She won't meet my eyes.

"You're serious."

She nods, suddenly very interested in the peace sign she is drawing with a broken pine branch in the sand.

I turn to Bert. "You knew about this?"

He shrugs. "It's in the Rules and Regulations."

Coralee clears her throat. "To officially kick off the pageant, all the girls get up onstage and sing the, um, pageant anthem together."

I raise my eyebrows so high, my sunglasses slip right off my head.

"And what is the pageant 'anthem,' exactly?"

"Oh, I don't remember it off the top of my head," Coralee says. *Liar.*

I grab my wheels. "Sing it or I'm out of here."

She stands and clears her throat so fast it's obvious she was just waiting to be asked. She pauses to sweep her hair back from her face. Then she starts doing some sort of vocal exercise that involves deep breathing and humming through her nose.

"Come *on*, already."

"Fine! But remember, you didn't let me fully warm up." She points at me. "You're getting the rough cut." And then she sings:

"When I wish upon a dream,
I can see the world, it seems,
In the distance shining bright
With our eternal flame of light.

Little Misses shine our light,
Share the love with all our might
Until the world in beauty unites.
We can share the love,
We can share the love.

Little Misses,
We can share the *love*."

Somewhere halfway through, Coralee closes her eyes. When she hits the last "love," she draws it out as long as a person can without expiring. Then she opens her eyes and looks at me and Bert. "Oh, close your mouth, you're catching flies."

Even Bert, master of the neutral response, is at a loss for words. Finally he comes out with, "It could, uh, use some tweaking on the rhyme scheme, but the sentiment is nice, I suppose."

I turn to him. "United in *beauty*? You approve of that?"

He nods. "If personality, intellect, emotional depth, and social kindness are taken into account as part of what makes a person beautiful, then yes. I would like to see a world where we are united in celebration of those things."

Coralee high-fives him. "That's what I'm *talking* about. But do you think I hit the second verse hard enough?"

The two bend their heads toward each other as Bert begins to give notes. I roll backward a bit, into the shadow of the pines, and look out over the quiet, blue depths of the lake. *This* is beauty. The natural world is always beautiful. People never criticize a rock for its roundness or a squirrel for its tail or a mountain for the shape of its peak. I wish I could say the same for humans.

Bert is attempting to sing the end of the second verse for Coralee so she can time the rhythm when Jackson and Cole, two kids who I spent all of seventh grade avoiding, come strolling down the beach shirtless with towels around their necks, nose-deep in their phones. Lord, please let the Wi-Fi be strong enough to pull their attention away from us.

Five feet away, where the path winds toward the parking lot, Cole looks up, his ferrety brown eyes right on Bert. My shoulders tighten. I had government with him last year. He spent the entire time attempting to explain to me why "women are the weaker sex" is actually a compliment.

Bert is belting out, "With our eternal flame of light," while staring at his watch to time it. So he does *not* see the moment Cole clocks him as potential summer fun. But I do. Cole nudges Jackson. They hold up their phones. Bert is seconds away from total social destruction.

I try to roll in front of him to block their view, but my chair gets stuck on a branch and my voice has gone into hiding somewhere in the back of my throat. Bert gets all the way through, "Little Misses, we can share the love," before I can bump him and let out a croak of warning, too little too late. His satchel falls to the sand.

"Hey!" he says to me right as Cole erupts in a fake laugh so high, I'm pretty sure only dogs can hear it. He's working it so hard it looks painful, but Jackson joins in anyway, flipping his hair back from his forehead like the surfer kid he wishes he was. They both start clapping.

"Nice one, Roberta. I knew you had it in you," Cole says, mid-applause.

Unlike me, who is still stuck in the sand, Coralee is in their faces in three steps. She grabs Jackson's phone, because he's closer and also the slower of the two. "Delete it."

Cole smirks. "Sure thing, Coralee. Let me just post it real quick, and we'll be on our way." His thumbs move over his phone and my insides clench.

"Touch that screen and this phone's going in the lake," Coralee threatens.

"What?" Jackson says, looking over at Cole for help.

Cole shakes his head. "You wouldn't. You don't got enough money to replace a new iPhone, *Beach Bum*."

She draws her arm back behind her head. "Try me."

Jackson punches Cole in the arm. "Delete it, man." Cole doesn't move. He's locked in a glare-off with Coralee, his face getting redder and redder.

He looks like he could hurt someone. Like actually hurt someone. If he touches Coralee . . . It's ninety degrees, but my insides go icy. I rock forward in the sand.

"Actually," Bert says, standing and walking toward them. I muscle my way forward right behind him. "Could I see that before you delete it?"

The air crackles, electric with tension, like right before

lightning strikes. I stop breathing. The sounds of the lake fade out. There is Cole and there is Coralee and nothing else.

Then Cole breaks his gaze to look over Coralee's shoulder at Bert.

"Why?"

"Because film is the most effective way to study yourself objectively," he explains. Everybody, including Coralee, turns to stare at him. The lapping water and shimmering waves come back into focus. I take a deep, shuddery breath. I have no idea what Bert is rambling about, but it's enough to cut the moment. Everybody, including Coralee, turns to stare at him. "I would like to know if the last note is a touch too high." He lowers his sunglasses so they sit on the tip of his nose and holds out his hand, palm up. "May I?"

Cole shakes his head, all the fight sucked out of him. "Forget it, man." He swipes left and then holds up the phone so we can all see the video is gone. Coralee quickly does the same with Jackson's phone and then tosses it back.

"Byeeeeee," she calls, and they walk away from us, shoulders hunched, up the path toward the parking lot, where Jackson's mom pulls up in a white Honda.

I swivel toward Bert as he pushes his sunglasses up,

walks back to his chair, sits, and takes a long sip from his Yeti. Coralee and I park ourselves at his feet.

"Now, where were we?" he says, picking up his clipboard.

"Uh, we were rehearsing the anthem," I remind him.

"Right. Well, let's proceed, shall we?" He holds out his satchel for me to clean. His hand shakes slightly, the only sign he's stressed. I wipe off the sand and place the satchel gently over the arm of his chair. Forget the pageant and everybody else. Bert is the most beautiful person on the planet.

10

An Unreasonable Request

Dear Deb Perelman at smittenkitchen.com,

It's been a while! Thank you for taking the time to write back to me when I told you how much our family loves your challah. You are the first and only chef who has answered one of my emails, and I will never forget it. And thank you for asking about my grandpa. He's doing all right. Alzheimer's isn't something you get better from, but he's happy at his new place and so we're happy for him.

Anyway, today I'm writing to thank you for another one of your recipes that has become a family favorite over here, but you'll never guess what it is. For one thing, it's savory, and for another, it's not even something you bake! My mema's most requested dish of yours is your black bean confetti salad. Now that they live over at Autumn Leaves, she's really missing her own garden, so I've been making your salad with all the onions and peppers she grew when she lived here. That way, she can have a taste of home.

I love how food can do that—send you back to a place you've been missing just by the taste of it. My mom got married recently and she's away on her honeymoon, and I've been missing her more than I'd like to admit. I wish there were a food that could send you back to a person. Now THAT would be magic.

Your ever-grateful fan,
Ellie Cowan

"Dad!" I yell from the back porch into the garage, where he has set up a card table and his laptop. He has fully given up pretending not to work and created a whole office in the garage, right alongside Grandpa's old wood-working tools and dead car batteries. Meg is less than thrilled.

"Yeah?" he calls, wiping sweat from his forehead with a paper towel. He keeps a roll of them on his card table for that very reason. When I told him he should just come work inside in the air-conditioning, he winked and said something about "the sacrifices we make for a little peace and quiet." I didn't wink back. I know all about the sacrifices he's made to get away from family.

I roll toward him down the sidewalk, bumpy with shells that Mema pressed into the cement with her own two hands. "Can you take me to Autumn Leaves?"

He checks his watch.

"Forget it." I turn and start to move away.

"No, no! I can do that! Give me five minutes, okay?" he says, and I nod without looking back. Mom never makes me feel like she's doing me a favor when I need her help.

When it's time to go, I tell Dad I want him to take Mom's van. I *don't* confess that it's because it has the lift and I'm too embarrassed to try to transfer into a regular seat again in front of him.

"You have to push the gray button on the key chain. No, the *other* gray button," I explain as the van beeps over and over, but the lift refuses to lower. He fiddles with it some more, muttering words Mom would never let me say, before handing me the keys.

"You do it."

I hit the correct button and hold it until the metal wheelchair lift lowers and hits the ground with a clang. I wheel myself on, but once I'm up and in the van, I have to direct Dad on how to latch down my chair. When it's finally done and we are cruising down Route 9 toward town, I keep my head turned toward the tar-covered cracks in the pavement to avoid Dad's eyes studying me in the rearview mirror. How is it that in all these years, he has never taken the time to learn to operate the *one* thing that gets his daughter from point A to point B?

"Well, look what the cat dragged in."

"You hate cats," I say to Mema when she bends down to give me a hug.

"But I love you, baby girl."

Mema and Grandpa's condo is on the first floor of Unit 4 on Maple Lane. All the areas in Autumn Leaves are divided up by the level of care the residents need, kind of like how it was whenever I had to go to the hospital. In the hospital, floor nine was intensive care, the highest floor and the highest level of care. It got easier and better as you worked your way down.

Residents on Maple Lane are mostly independent, but home-care nurses drop by to check on them every day. Mema and Grandpa used to live on Crabapple Street in Unit 3, but when he stopped remembering to get up in time to make it to the bathroom, they had to move here. On good days he jokes that he ought to get an old folks' discount on Pampers. On bad days he bats at the nurses and tries to lock himself in the bathroom. I hope today is a good day.

Mema looks over my shoulder as I sit on her front stoop with a plastic container of confetti salad in my lap. "Your daddy didn't want to drop in and say hi?" she asks, but doesn't look surprised. She knows what's up. As soon as I made it onto the curb, Dad hightailed it out of here with a promise to be back in an hour.

He is straight-up terrified of Mema. He can hardly be in a room with her without hiding behind his cell phone and jingling all the coins in his pockets. I'm pretty sure he's faked a few phone calls just to get away from her unblinking stare. I guess that's what happens when you have to face the mother of the woman you left without so much as a *see you later, alligator*. Every time Mom argues that he really is trying now, Mema turns her nose up like she's sniffed out a skunk and then pretends to be hard of hearing.

I hand her the confetti salad.

"My ugly dip!" she says, pulling me in for an even bigger hug.

"It's called confetti salad, Mema, you know that," I say into her shoulder.

"Nah, look at all those black beans and mushed-up bits of peppers. It's ugly as sin, but I love it."

I follow her into her kitchen, which is smaller than the one in the trailer, if that's even possible. A pan soaks in the sink, and the air smells like crispy fried okra.

"I guess y'all already ate dinner. You can just stick that in the fridge for later if you want." I point at the salad.

Mema shakes her head. "Salad for dessert sounds just about perfect." She passes me a bag of Fritos. "Open that for me, will ya? And then let's take our treats out back to the patio. Your grandpa's resting."

Their little square of pavement behind the condo has a view of the pond. I watch the geese traipse up and down the lawn with their giant black feet.

"He having a good day?" I ask through a mouthful of chip and dip.

"As good as any," Mema answers, which could mean anything. I'd lean over and give her another hug, but that would make three since I came in the door, and any number over two gets her bristling with suspicion. She is wary of anyone who might be feeling sorry for her. I recognize the sentiment.

"So," she says, leaning back in her chair and crossing her arms over her checkered blue shirt. Her Keds are the exact same shade. "To what do I owe the pleasure of this visit? Don't tell me you were missin' your old grandma. It hasn't gotten *that* bad over there, has it?" She smiles, but there's real fear in her voice. She would have moved back in a heartbeat to stay with me while Mom was gone. But she couldn't leave Grandpa, and Grandpa can't leave this place, and this place is residents only, so we Cowan women are now many links in a chain that stretches out across the state of Oklahoma.

"Nah. Dad's okay. I'm good," I lie, because I don't want her to worry and also because I am about to ask her for a huge favor.

"Okay, then," she says, not believing me for one minute. "Then why are you here unexpectedly on a Wednesday evening with my favorite dip in the whole world?"

I shift in my chair. "Can't a girl just need her people?"

She raises an eyebrow at me. "A girl *can*. But in my experience, if a person unexpectedly comes bearing food, they're either about to give you bad news or they need something from you."

"Well, it's not bad news."

She starts rocking in her chair. "Mm-hmm. Out with it."

I take a deep breath and say it as fast as I can before I chicken out. "I need to borrow seventy-five dollars, but I promise I will pay it back!"

Mema stops rocking. "Seventy-five dollars for what?"

"Here's the part you're not gonna like."

"You mean besides the fact that I'll be seventy-five bucks poorer?"

"Yeah, besides that. I can't exactly tell you why I need it."

Mema shakes her head. "A request without a reason is not a reasonable request, my girl."

I fiddle with the chip in my hand and try not to panic. Once her mind's made up, it takes a mountain and a miracle to change it. My window of opportunity is closing by the second. But I can't tell her it's to enter a beauty pageant, because then she'll tell Mom, and Mom has always said, from the beginning of time, that anyone who judges you on your outward appearance is not worth knowing. She would drive all the way back from wherever the heck she is right now just to lecture me on society's toxic beauty standards. Then she would ground me for all of eternity.

"It's so I can do a favor for a friend!" I yelp.

Mema leans forward and stares into my eyes like the human lie detector she is. "This a good friend?"

"Yes, ma'am. The *best*," I say, picturing Coralee knocking at my window, ready to cheer me up after Mom left, and standing in her pink bikini with Jackson's phone high in the air, ready to send it to the depths to save Bert.

Mema blinks. I must have passed. I eat my chip.

"All right, then. But you have to promise to tell me what all this is about after the fact." She takes another bite of confetti-salad-slash-ugly-dip. "I'm a sucker for a good adventure tale."

Behind us, the glass door slides open and Grandpa walks out in a pair of wrinkled shorts and his undershirt. "Ellie, my darlin', just in time for magic hour!" he says, and sweeps his hand out toward the lawn and the pond, where the sun has begun to set, throwing a peachy soft glow over everything.

"How you feeling, Grandpa?" I ask as he does a little two-step shuffle toward us.

"Oh, right as rain, Ellie girl, now that you're here," he says, and steals a chip.

Mema smiles at me over his shoulder. I just found my registration fee and my grandpa remembered my name. It *is* magic hour.

11

Little Misses

Hello, Ellie!

Greetings from Sapulpa, home of the Heart of Route 66 Auto Museum, where you can not only view 10,000 square feet of antique cars but also see the World's Tallest Gas Pump! The things you do for love.

I'm kidding. I actually think you would have gotten a kick out of the museum. I've never seen so much chrome, and the car guys who volunteer there couldn't get enough of the pictures I showed them of you changing out the casters on your wheelchair. They said they'd make you an honorary mechanic.

That is, if I could drag you away from Meadow Blackberry Farm. El, you would have been in heaven: 2,300 blackberry plants, and we hit it at peak season! We filled so many baskets, we had to give most of them away at the RV park so we could pull out the bed. We were the hit of the park! Oh, but the best part, Ellie, was the black-berry hand pies we ate on the farm. They were still warm and sprinkled with that big crackly sugar you love. I got them to print out the recipe so you could try it at home!

Love you, my girl! Write soon, okay?

Xoxoxoxo,

Mom

Wow. So many exclamation points. This is what hap-pens when I don't email for a few days. The problem with having one gigantic secret that you can't talk about is that it makes it hard to talk at all. Every time I sit down to write, I end up rambling about the squirrels on the roof and the heat index. So I hit delete. If I write about the weather, she'll know something's up for sure.

I set the phone facedown on my bedside table and pull a Ping-Pong ball from the jar. Number one: *Smell something new.* Oh, well, that's easy: the Neutrogena self-tanning lotion Coralee brought over yesterday to do a test patch on me to see if I'd break out. Good news— no breakout! Bad news—my arm from wrist to elbow is the color of rotting orange peel now. When Patrick saw it, he ran screaming from the dinner table. Dad did not ask, which is where we're at right now. Dad doesn't ask where I am most days, and I don't ask why he's hiding in the garage instead of hanging with his family on *family* vacation. Win-win. The tanning lotion smells like burnt hair.

Outside, a horn honks and then keeps honking in one long, painful whine. I am down the hall and almost to the door when Dad intercepts me, pulling back the curtains from the window and frowning. The *one* time he's not in his garage office.

"Hi, Dad! Bye, Dad!" I say, angling past him.

"Off again?" The answer is so obvious, I don't even nod.

But I can't get my wheels past him to reach the door. Instead of escaping, I have to sit here and stare up at him as he stares at my getaway car. In the driveway, the horn honker has found some kind of rhythm and is tapping it out with increasing speed. Oh no. I recognize it. It's the Little Miss Boots and Bows anthem. Coralee must be fully caffeinated.

"Can I, ummm?" I tilt my head toward the door, hands itching to wheel myself out of here.

"Where . . . ? When . . . ?" He wants to ask so many things, but he isn't sure if it's his place to do it. I blink up at him innocently. Finally he steps back and opens the door. I roll out and suck in the muggy, sticky air. Freedom!

"Back in a couple of hours!" I call over my shoulder.

Susie doesn't even try to parallel park this time when we pull up in front of the Rocking Horse Theater. Instead, before we've even come to a full stop, she flicks on her hazards and pops the trunk so Bert can get my chair. Bert informed me on the way here that there would be several of these rehearsals, though he wouldn't commit to a number, which is highly suspect coming from him. I thought this was a one-and-done kind of thing. Apparently, Coralee knew all along and "forgot" to tell me. First the anthem, then this. Coralee is just *full* of surprises.

"I'll be over at Timely Treasures, the thrift shop down the street, hunting for some cookware," Susie calls through the open window. "Y'all come find me when you're done!"

We wave goodbye as she drives off, leaving us in the fog of the Caddy's exhaust without so much as a glance in the rearview mirror.

"She's touchy today," Coralee explains as Bert coughs once into the crook of his arm. "The drugstore was out of gum *and* her patches. They said they can't get either until next week."

It's going to be a long ride home.

We turn back toward the theater, which looks even worse in the midday heat than it did last time. The marquee says it had a showing of *Roman Holiday* last night, PLUS A FREE PERSONAL PIZZA WITH EVERY TICKET! The glass doors are smeared with grease. We hold our noses past the lobby because the whole place smells like old cheese. Even the blast of Febreze from the restrooms can't compete.

Once we are in the auditorium, it's just the same as last time, barely anyone here. If this is the rehearsal for our age group, Coralee's got this in the bag. Bert is clearly thinking the same thing. He's grinning like the Cheshire cat.

We move down the aisle to the front, where Rae Ann Perkins, former Little Miss 1986, rushes over to us. Her helmet of hair is once again impeccable. She could bike ride and be totally safe. Today she has exchanged her skirt and blazer for a terrifyingly tight pair of leopard-print leggings and matching tank top.

"Hello, Mrs. Perkins," Coralee says in a voice so polite I turn to see if it's really her.

"You came!" Rae Ann says, rushing past Coralee and kneeling in front of me. The four blond girls onstage stop their stretching to see what the commotion is about.

"Uh, yeah. Here you go." I thrust the envelope at her with seventy-five dollars in cash, courtesy of Mema. When she moves to take it, I have to order my fingers to release. "It's all there," I add unnecessarily, since she tucks it under her arm without counting it.

"Right this way, ladies!" she trills, finally gracing Coralee with a smile, which sends my friend into what I can only describe as car-bobblehead nodding. She dips her head in gratitude and then dips it again until she can't seem to stop. I bump my wheel into her shin and she stills.

"Now, don't worry," Rae Ann says, turning back to me with her hands in the air. "I remember—look, don't touch, right?" She gestures to my chair. I bite back every single one of the zillion potential responses I could make to that question-that's-not-a-question, because they are all inappropriate. Instead I give her my fakest smile so she'll stop looking at me and get on with it already.

We follow her to the front of the stage, where she claps

her hands like a first-grade teacher. Please, no one ever give this woman a whistle. Bert takes his place in the first row of theater seats and opens his laptop with a professional clearing of his throat, while the rest of us gather at two of the round tables, which are sticky with bits of crunchy tomato sauce and shriveled pepperoni slices from last night's Italian-themed feast.

Coralee sits on my left, and the girl who was reading the book at registration claims the chair on my right. Rae Ann disappears around the side of the stage and then reappears from behind a curtain to take her place front and center so we can all look up at her like lemmings.

"Welcome, welcome, Little Misses. We are honored to have you here as shining examples of our fine state of Oklahoma!"

I suppress a shudder at both "Little Misses" and the fact that she is referring to herself in the plural form. Mema always says, *Beware the person who speaks with the royal "we."*

"Today, you will embark on one of the greatest and noblest journeys of your adolescence," she states.

I snicker and Coralee elbows me. But the girl to my right laughs under her breath too. I sneak a glance at her, hoping to catch her eye. She has a book under the table open to chapter five of *One for the Murphys*.

"Nice selection," I whisper, and risk a small smile. "I'm Ellie."

She whispers back, "Thanks. I'm Maya." When she gives me a quick grin, I smile wider. Maybe Coralee won't be my only ally here. Coralee jabs me in the arm so I'll pay attention. I want to poke her back and point out that I'm putting in an effort and making friends. She'd probably just say I'm socializing with the enemy.

Up onstage, Rae Ann has begun pacing back and forth with her hands behind her back like a tiny army general. "Now, I'm sure you girls already know all this, but let me give you a brief history lesson as to how the Little Miss Boots and Bows Pageant first began, way back in 1924. It was the roaring twenties and a glorious time of freedom and celebration for women everywhere. . . ."

I laugh again. How could I not? Maya nudges me, and we share an eye roll. I wait for Coralee's warning to *pay attention*, but she is staring up at Rae Ann with wide and unblinking eyes, like Rae Ann is imparting the secrets of the universe.

I rock back and forth on my wheels. I should have brought a book.

Seventeen agonizing minutes later, Rae Ann claps her hands again and calls us all over to the side of the stage, where a set of steps lead up to the top. A. Set. Of. Steps.

I prod Coralee and then point to the stairs. Her eyes go wide. It is the first time today she gives me her full attention.

The other girls hop nimbly up the stairs like wood sprites. Coralee leans over and says, "Okay, there's got to be a way we can do this. I'll carry your chair and you can just—"

"Just what, Coralee? Scoot up the stairs on my butt for the world to see? Forget it. I'm out." I reverse away from her, and to her credit, she doesn't try to stop me. But how could she even *suggest* carrying my chair while everybody watches? I'm mad, embarrassed, frustrated. I am *all the things*. It sucks all the air out of the room. I have to go, *now*.

"Hold on, dear!" Rae Ann calls from the stage.

The last thing I plan to do is "hold on." I race over to Bert. "Let's get out of here."

He nods without question and begins to stand. But he's not fast enough for Rae Ann.

"Yoo-hoo! Ellie, dear!" she calls from the top of the stage. "Don't worry, I haven't forgotten about you!" *If only*. Then she disappears behind the curtain only to pop up again at the bottom of the stairs like the world's worst Whack-a-Mole. She is struggling to hold up what appears to be a large, very heavy sheet of metal. Against my better judgment, I roll forward to see what she's got. And then as soon as I see it, I want to propel myself right back out of here at warp speed.

It's a wheelchair ramp. The woman has hauled in a portable wheelchair ramp.

"Now, you probably know how to do this better than me." She begins to set it down, but it's awkward and the corner gets stuck on one of the stairs. She stands and her back makes an audible pop. She is willing to break herself in half rather than let me bow out of her precious pageant. Also, why does she think I'd know any better than her how to set that thing up? Does the fact that I'm in a wheelchair automatically mean I know the ins and outs of every single mobility device in production? No, ma'am.

Coralee rushes forward to help her, ignoring my glare. Between the two of them, they manage to set the ramp over the stairs so that it reaches from the floor to the stage without a gap.

"Voilà!" Rae Ann says, dusting off her hands like she put in a hard day's work.

I roll to the bottom of the ramp, my face on fire. Everybody else is already onstage. Everybody but me and my chair. Maya is the only one with the grace not to stare as I study the ramp. It looks too steep. Way too steep for me to muscle my way up. I'm stronger than I've ever been, thanks to Hutch's exercises and a growth spurt last year. I can transfer from bed to chair and chair to car. I can navigate down dirt roads and over sand. I can pop wheelies all day. But I *cannot* defy gravity.

But the part of me that likes a challenge convinces the part of me that uses common sense to give it a go. I will not let this woman make me feel like I am less capable than anyone else.

I back up a few feet to get some leverage and push as hard and as fast as I can toward the ramp.

I sense the wrongness of the angle before my wheels even hit. I take the edge too sharply and am jerked backward. I catch myself at the last second before I topple over, but I can't say the same for the ramp. It tips sideways and slides off the steps with a deafening clang. Up onstage, a few girls gasp and Rae Ann rushes over. "Oh honey, oh honey, I am so sorry! Are you all right?"

I can't answer. My heart beats like a trapped bird, searching for a way out.

I sense Bert behind me before I see him. He leans down and whispers so only I can hear, "I believe the exits are back and to the right. Would you like me to escort you?" I nod and turn, following the sound of his sneakers squeaking on the theater floor because I can't summon the courage to lift my head. It's the roll of shame. Except *they* should be ashamed, not me—Rae Ann and Coralee and all of them with their deep looks of concern and not one ounce of understanding.

Outside, the world carries on as usual. Bert sits on the curb next to a planter filled with dead petunias, and I park myself next to him. When I sniff, Bert offers me a Kleenex from his pocket.

"I hate pageants," I say.

"I know," he responds.

"I quit."

"You should," he says.

I'm so surprised I forget I'm upset.

"I *should*?"

He nods, hugging his satchel in his lap. "It's clear this pageant is not equipped to handle someone with a physical disability. They are in violation of at least seven American Disability Act laws, not to mention the discriminatory behavior of the pageant coordinator herself."

I wince. Everything he says is right, of course. Mom would lose her mind if I told her even one-tenth of what happened here today. But hearing it out loud makes me feel worse.

A shadow falls over us both.

"Can I join you?" It's Maya, with her book in hand.

Bert scoots over, and she sits between us. I smile, but all I can think is, *Where is Coralee?*

"Maya Sinclair, pageant contestant," she says to Bert.

"Bert Akers, manager," he says. They shake hands.

She stretches out her long legs and says, matter-of-factly, "This pageant is a joke."

"So why are you doing it?" I ask.

She raises an eyebrow at me. "Why are *you*?"

Good question. "Because my friend is in it and she asked me to do it with her—Coralee, with the blond hair."

She smirks. "Which one?"

I cackle. It feels good, and she's got a point. "The one in the green tights and purple sweatband." *The one who still hasn't come out here to check on me.*

"I see. Well, I'm doing this for practice," Maya explains.

Bert turns to her, intrigued. "Practice for what?"

"The Bee," she says like it's a thing I should know.

"*The* Bee?" he gasps, like the entire word should be capitalized. Apparently it *is* a thing I should know.

"That's right," she says, and a moment of silence falls over them both as they contemplate the bigness of THE BEE.

"Ummm, the what, now?" I ask, because their little moment is making me lonelier than I already was.

"The Scripps National Spelling Bee," Bert answers in wonder.

"I can spell anything." The way Maya says it leaves no room for doubt. "And I can study, make flash cards, take online tutorials for speed. But I can't simulate a live contest." She shrugs. "The pageant is the best way to prepare for the public pressure."

Bert is nodding vigorously. "Flawless logic," he says, and then blushes when she shoots him a grin.

"Well, I, for one, don't need any more pressure. Bert"—I nudge him with my elbow so he'll remember I'm there—"you want to head toward Timely Treasures and see if we can wait out the rest of rehearsal there?"

Bert manages to tear his eyes away from Maya long enough to nod at me, but before we start moving, the doors behind us open and Coralee bursts out. *Finally.* Sometimes it takes Coralee a minute, but when she eventually realizes it, she admits when she's wrong. I turn to face her.

"I fixed it!" She shimmies up to me with a mile-wide smile. *I'm sorry, what?* "Turns out Rae Ann borrowed that ramp from the old folks' home near her house. So *I* suggested she go back and check for a longer one. Next time you'll be able to make it up, easy peasy!" She clasps her hands and looks excitedly from me to Maya to Bert. When no one moves, she looks back to me.

"What?"

"Coralee, I am not going back in there."

"Well, of course not. Rehearsal's over for today anyway. We have until next week to memorize the anthem and practice interview questions! This was just a teensy bump."

"No. Not a teensy bump. A huge bump, Coralee. A Mount Everest bump. I'm not going back in there *ever*."

I roll down the sidewalk in the direction that Susie's car disappeared and away from Coralee. She doesn't get it. I'm not quitting because of the ramp. I'm quitting because a roomful of people just saw me crash and burn, and I don't care to be around those people anymore. Also, I should never have had to be around them in the *first* place.

She jogs to catch up with me and then runs in front so I have to stop or run her over. I'm tempted.

"I'm sorry! Okay?" she says. "I am the worst. I dragged you into this and it turned into a disaster, but"—she runs her hands through her hair, sending her sweatband askew—"I'm trying to fix it."

I study her. We have been best friends for more than a year and a half now. I can tell when she's lying and when she really means it. This time, she means it. I just wish the "it" she's trying to fix isn't about me and my wheelchair. But then I remember the look on Dad's face when

I mentioned the pageant. He didn't think I could do it because of my chair. If I quit now, I'm proving him right. At least Coralee believes in me.

"Fine." I plug my ears against her screams of joy. "But if that woman adds choreography, I will revolt. I mean it. I have successfully avoided every middle school dance thus far, and that will not change now. Rae Ann will just have to deal with it."

"Singing only. Got it!" She dives in for a hug. It is a very sweaty, very clingy hug. But I hug her back, because in the five minutes that she was inside and I was outside with Bert and Maya on the curb, I missed her more than I will ever admit.

12

Yellow Sticker Day

The bell on the door over the Timely Treasures thrift shop jingles cheerily when Coralee hurls it open and runs in like she's crossing the finish line at a marathon. She's riding high now that we're all, as she likes to put it, "back in the game." I let Bert and Maya go ahead of me. Coralee might be chanting "Operation Boots and Bows is a go!" but I'm in no hurry to celebrate. Because now I really *do* have to get up on that stage and answer questions about my life and twirl around in a dress.

The dress factor is why we're here in the first place. None of us has much money, Maya included. She explained on the way over that all available cash goes to books, a budgeted plan that Bert wholeheartedly endorsed.

So now we're thumbing through the racks of second- and third- and fourth-hand clothes in a low-ceilinged room that smells a little like the canning shed. Susie has her pile of cookware up at the register, but she doesn't seem to be in a hurry. I have no excuse to get out of shopping—my least favorite activity on the planet. I would watch Mema's favorite dog show over this. Actually, those dogs with all their bows and conditioner are probably better groomed than me.

The girl at the counter, with tattoos stretching down both arms, does not look up from the giant textbook in front of her when she says, "Dressing room's that closet in the back. Hang 'em up after you try 'em." The squeak of her highlighter and the whirring of the overhead fans are the only sounds in this place.

I squeeze down an overcrowded aisle until I am alone at the end of the row in the dim light from a too-high window. I like it in here. It might be musty and dark, but it's comforting, like a blanket pulled over my head. Basically, the opposite of the Rocking Horse Theater.

"Check this out!" Coralee squeals, ducking into my aisle of clothes from the next one over with an actual tiara perched on her head. It's a thin circle of silver studded with green and purple and pink rhinestones in the shapes of flowers. She takes it off and tosses it to me. It's light as air—a perfect plastic tiara. I put it on my head. She snaps a photo with her trusty camera.

"See, you're already a queen," she says, showing me the image on her screen. The purple in the flowers matches the purple on my chair. My hair lies as straight as always except for one strand that has fallen across my sunburned nose. I look like a fairy queen in a forest of vintage wear.

"I love it," I say, and I do. "But we're here for the clothes." I hand the tiara back to her, brushing the flowers with my fingers one last time. And then I throw up some spirit fingers and force some cheer. "I want to see you in your Sunday best!"

She cackles and dances off. Maybe this won't be so bad.

An hour later and it is exactly that bad. Coralee argues with Susie over three eighties prom dresses that she cannot *possibly* live without. Maya models a blue sleeveless floor-length dress that shows off her broad shoulders and long hair. Bert adjusts a straw fedora that he claims will complete his "summer look." But me? I can't even find a skirt that isn't covered in ruffles or so short it'd be borderline indecent as I sit in my chair. When your main goal is easy movement, comfort will always come before fashion.

But—and I would never confess this out loud, especially to Mom, whose mantra is "Beauty comes from the inside out, not the other way around"—I want to feel good when I get onstage. It's going to be hard enough to make myself smile and play along. A great dress would make it a teensy bit easier.

I'm in the very last aisle with a pile of discarded dresses in my lap and no options left, when Audrey, the girl from the front desk, comes out of the closet-sized dressing room with a handful of clothes draped over her arm.

"Hold on," I say, pointing to the one on top. "Can I see that?"

"This?" she says, holding up the dress she was in the process of putting back on its hanger. She shrugs. "Sure."

I take it from her and hang it facing out on the rack next to me so I can see it better. It's sleeveless with a seam running right down the middle. One side is bright blue with a white pocket. The other side is the reverse—white with a blue pocket—so that it looks like two pieces of a mismatched puzzle. The blue is the color of the Oklahoma sky on a cloudless day when it stretches forever in all directions. Blue and white polka dots cover the round collar. I love it immediately. But I hold my breath until I can try it on.

The dressing room is barely big enough to fit my chair, and it doesn't have a mirror, so if I want to see myself, I have to roll all the way to the floor-length mirror at the front of the store. I manage to wriggle myself into the dress. *Do* I want to see myself? I feel the fabric on my legs. It's soft and stretchy and airy. The collar is loose and lies flat. I stick my hands in the pockets. It feels right. But I still don't know how it looks.

I take three deep breaths and nudge the door open with my knee. Then I roll slowly down the aisle toward the mirror, taking more deep breaths and telling myself that if this doesn't work out, it's not the end of the world, because why do I care anyway if I look good in a pageant I don't even want to win?

But when I get closer, almost to the end of the aisle and the front where the mirror looms, I realize I *do* care, and I can't make myself look. Pretty isn't a thing I've ever really wanted to feel. My goal was to get people to *stop* looking at me, not the other way around.

I start to retreat back down the aisle. I'll wear the peach dress Mema made for the wedding. It'll be fine. It'll be enough to meet the "Rules and Regulations." Then I can go back to my normal life.

I almost make it. Then I hear the whistle—the long, high-pitched, two-fingers-in-the-mouth piercing cry that is Coralee's calling card. I freeze and close my eyes, because I know what's coming—an unstoppable train of Spandex and enthusiasm.

"Whoa, baby, check you *out*!" she calls, her flip-flops slapping down the aisle.

"Really?" I say, peeking at her with one eye as she stands in front of me. I want to see if she means it or if she's just doing that over-the-top, this-is-the-best-thing-in-my-entire-life routine she does about everything from ice cream sandwiches to pink gel pens.

She crosses both of her hands over her heart. "Really. But don't listen to me. Come look at yourself."

I roll a little more quickly with Coralee by my side toward the mirror next to the front counter. Bert and Maya and Susie wait by the register with their purchases in recycled Walmart bags. They all watch me approach, and a wave of nerves ripples through me that I know is just a taste of whatever I'll experience when I get up onstage with all those eyes on me. At least here I am among friends.

I spin toward the mirror.

There I am. Still me. But whatever material the dress is made out of shimmers under the flickering overhead light. The blue-on-white and white-on-blue is almost a pattern, but not. Almost predictable, but not. It's not cutesy. No one will ever say *aren't you the sweetest thing* to me in this dress. It's . . . cool. I watch myself smile.

Audrey comes out from behind the counter and sizes me up. "Needs a bit of altering," she says with her hands on her hips, "but, yeah, not everybody can pull that look off. Sixties mod suits you."

"Thanks." I don't know what "sixties mod" means, but it sounds like a compliment, so I'll take it.

She walks between me and the mirror to check the tag. "Yellow sticker. Even better. That's fifty percent off today."

I smile wider. I guess sometimes it's good to be seen.

13

False Starts

Dear Ellie,

I met a bull named Beauregard! I even touched him on the nose! I think this honeymoon is making me braver, or maybe it's RV brain. Is that a thing? Like cabin fever? I haven't had a proper shower in two and a half weeks. I miss our bathroom. I miss a toilet you don't have to empty yourself. I miss a bed that doesn't fold out. But when we camp under the stars, oh honey, you cannot beat it. It's like God poked holes in the universe just for us. I promise to take you someday. I want you to see all this wide-open beauty with your own eyes.

As for Beauregard, we met him at the rodeo here in Arcadia. He was sweet, like Ferdinand. I should warn you, though, we have a new addition to our family. His name is Beau Jr. and he is small and yellow and Jim won him in a ring toss. Do you remember Nugget, the goldfish you got at the fair when you were little? Probably not. He only made it ten days. Let's hope Beau Jr. lasts a little longer.

Love you so, so, so, so, so much,
Mom

Dear Mom,

Sorry it's been a few days since I've written. Wow! A bull AND a goldfish. Livin' life on the edge. Give Beauregard Jr. my best regards (pun intended) and try not to kill him for the next ten days so I can at least see him when you get home.

Life is goodish here. Everyone's still alive. I, too, am livin' on the edge. I went—wait for it—shopping! That's right, your girl bought a dress. But this is a one-off. Don't start planning marathon mall visits for when you get home.

I pulled number four in the Lotto today, so I suppose that's my "see something new"—me, in a dress of my own choosing.

Love, love, love you,

Me

I reread my email and then hit send. No need to tell Mom *why* I went shopping for a dress or what I plan to use it for. Let her be happy that I am branching out. More importantly, I am not lying in a heap in the sewing-machine corner, missing her. It took me five days to even get up the courage to tell her about the shopping. So much has happened since she's been gone. It's not like I'm a totally new Ellie, but I'm definitely not the one she left. I entered a pageant, almost quit a pageant, made a new friend in Maya, bought a dress I actually like, tolerated Dad.

"Ellie? May I come in?" Speaking of Dad.

My bedroom door is open, and as I look over, Dad sticks his head in. I do a double take, because on that head is a tan canvas hat covered in . . . feathers.

I point. "Uh, are you going on safari?"

"Nope." When he shakes his head, the feathers flutter.

"Training to be Big Bird?"

He steps into the room and tips his feathery hat to me. "No, Ellie, my dear. *This* is a fishing hat." He unhooks a feather and hands it to me. It's a fishing lure. One of Grandpa's old fishing lures. Dad must have found them in the garage. I'm pretty sure there are still worm guts on here. I set it carefully on my bedside table, as far away from me as it can go.

"So you're going fishing?" Meg must have threatened to take away his laptop if he didn't stop working.

"Correction," he says, removing the hat and plopping it on my head. "*We* are going fishing—you, me, Meg, and the boys."

The last person I went fishing with was Grandpa, and that was at least three years ago, before he stopped being able to drive a car, much less a boat.

"Do you, um, know how to fish?" I ask.

He stares at me, his dark hair rumpled from the hat, and then he starts laughing like I just said the funniest thing in the world. "Oh, Ellie. Have a little *faith*. Meet me in the driveway in fifteen minutes," he says, and backs out.

He did not actually answer my question.

Fifteen minutes later, I am parked in the driveway as ordered, holding the water chair I use for canoeing and kayaking in my lap. Meg stands next to me, wrestling the boys to the ground with a tube of sunscreen. But Dad? Dad is nowhere to be seen.

"So," I say to Meg, when she releases the boys, who are off like gunshots toward the sprinkler in the garden, their limbs shiny with Coppertone. "Did my dad rent a boat from the marina?"

"What?" she says, her words muffled by her hands as she rubs sunscreen onto her own face. "No, he's using the fishing boat. You know, your grandfather's boat?"

I must have misheard her. There's no way that could be right. Grandpa's boat hasn't seen water since he last put it in the lake himself. It's been abandoned under a blue tarp at the back of the garden long enough for the blackberry vines to make it part of their fence.

At that very moment, when I am about to point out the impossibility of what Meg has just told me, I hear the rumbling of an engine. Then Dad's giant black Suburban rolls around the corner of the house from the direction of the garden—with Grandpa's fishing boat trailing behind.

I keep my face neutral as he smiles and waves out the window like he is returning from overseas. I've never in my entire life even seen Dad on the water. I'm not entirely sure Grandpa's boat is still usable. I've never seen Patrick and Finn sit still for more than thirty seconds unless an electronic device was involved. Not to mention the part that involves me getting from land onto the water. There are so many things wrong with this plan. Strangely, my last thought as he pulls up in a cloud of dust and good intentions is, *If I drown today, I won't get to wear my new dress.*

We ride to No. 9 landing in silence. The transfer into the Suburban from my chair was brutal. The seat is at least a foot higher off the ground than the one in Susie's Cadillac, so it took me several tries to get in while the boys fought over their own spots in the back and Dad fiddled with the trailer. I wish we had taken the van. But there's no way it could have hauled the boat. The mammoth Suburban can barely tow it. Also, I don't think Dad hooked the hitch up right. The trailer squeaks and whines. Every turn, I check behind us to make sure it's still there. Through it all, Dad wears his hat, feathers dangling in front of his eyes.

When we get to the slipway, Dad makes everybody get out so Meg can shout directions as he backs the trailer into the water.

"No! Left. *My* left!" she shouts. It doesn't make a difference. Dad ignores her instructions. Instead he leans out the open window, steers with one hand, and tries to do it all by himself. A few kayakers eating granola bars and playing cards on the rocks stop to watch.

The sun is a magnifying glass and I am the ant. It's just past lunch—peak time for sunstroke. Any good fisher hits the lake in the early hours when the air is cool and the fish are chipper. Dad would know this if he had clocked more hours on the water instead of on his laptop. The heat soaks into my bones, and sweat runs slick down my thighs against my chair. It doesn't help that I am wearing a swimsuit and shorts and a T-shirt *and* my life vest, because Meg made us all put them on the minute we got out of the car so we wouldn't forget them.

Twenty minutes and one scratched bumper later, the boat is afloat. Dad stands knee-deep in the lake, wiping sweat off his face and plastering on a grin.

"All right, family! Everybody in!" And there it is. The one piece of the puzzle he hasn't thought out. My heart lurches forward and then shudders to a stop. It takes him until Finn and Patrick clamber up over the sides to realize I cannot get "in" unless he carries me—something *I* have not stopped thinking about since he popped his head into my room an hour ago and suggested this whole thing.

"Greg," Meg says, and tilts her head toward me. I feel like the last unclaimed bag on the carousel. He looks at me, pauses for a fraction of a second, and then wades back toward the shore. I swallow, my throat scratchy. I want a drink of water and to be anywhere else on the planet.

"So, behind the back and under the knees?" he asks, his arms outstretched. *Lord, please don't let him drop me.*

"Meg, will you take my water chair?" I ask, handing her the folded seat. With a voice as steady as I can make it and without looking at Dad, I explain how she has to set it up in the boat.

Once the chair is in place and Meg and the boys are in place and basically everybody else in the world is in their place, I lean forward and put my arms around Dad's slippery neck. Our faces are so close I have to turn away so we don't bump noses. I can smell his coffee breath. His eyes are wide with fear. I shut my own because nothing would make this moment worse than to have to watch how terrified he is to handle me.

"Behind the back and under the knees," I repeat with a whisper.

"One, two, *three*." He lifts and thankfully, does not grunt.

We are to the boat in four quick strides. I strap myself into my seat without meeting anyone's gaze. Instead I stare out at the blinding lake, unblinking, until my eyes water. Dad, of course, has rallied. He perches himself on the edge of the last seat at the back of the boat by the motor and calls, "Drumroll, please!"

Meg beats a rhythm on the edge of the boat with her hands. Finn and Patrick stomp both their feet, rocking the boat so much that Dad has to tell everybody to stop. I'm too busy holding on to do much of anything.

He grabs the starter cord on the motor and says to me, "Wish me luck."

"Luck," I reply, because what else am I going to say?

He yanks his arm back as far as it will go. The motor makes a noise like an animal caught in a trap and then stops. He pulls again. Same sound, but shorter. And again. Until Dad is spewing so much profanity that Meg makes both boys cover their ears. Then she mutters a few choice words of her own.

The air smells of gasoline and burnt oil. We bob on the water a few feet from shore. The kayakers are long gone. The engine ticks. But still we sit. I watch Meg. Whatever happens next will be her call.

She takes a few deep breaths, the ruffled top of her tankini expanding with each one. Then she hands the boys their poles. "Right. This looks like the perfect fishing spot. Patrick, pass me the tackle box. Finn, get your finger out of your nose and keep the cork on your hook until I say otherwise."

She passes me my own pole, a Minnie Mouse relic Dad must have found in the garage along with the hat and other fishing gear. But before I can reach into the tackle box for a lure, Dad takes a giant step out of the boat and sends us swaying.

"Nope." He shakes his head, grabs the prow with both hands, and heaves. We jolt forward toward the shore. Finn drops his pole in the water and starts crying, and my water chair rocks so hard so I have to scramble to hold on to the side.

"Greg, stop!" Meg yells. "What are you doing?!"

He won't look at her. Instead he marches away from the boat and out of the water altogether and disappears around the front of the car. Without his cursing and the sound of the dying, now dead, motor, I can hear the lapping of the water on the hull. Far off, by the buoys, a seagull cries.

Dad is in the Suburban. The brake lights come on. Is he seriously going to leave us in a broken-down boat at the edge of the lake? But then the car begins to reverse, the trailer dipping back into the water until it is inches from the boat.

Dad jumps out again. He claps for the boys. "Get into this car right now." Patrick's wails join Finn's. Meg doesn't say a word, but she doesn't have to. If Meg were a bug zapper right now, Dad would be toast. She glances again toward me and then pointedly back at Dad.

"Right," he says, and heads back into the water. "We'll

do it in two. One"—he wraps his arms around me and looks away—"and *two*." I have just enough time to unclip myself from my seat and scrabble for his neck before I am up and over the water and in the car.

I grab the armrest as we speed away, rocks from the unpaved road ricocheting off the trailer on the hull of the boat. I should be grateful I didn't have to do another transfer from my wheelchair into the monster of a Suburban. But all I can think is, *Who is this guy right now?*

Back at the house, Dad is the first one out of the car. After unloading my wheelchair, he retreats to the garage. Meg stomps right in there after him. I take Finn and Patrick inside and set them up in front of the television with homemade yogurt pops to drown out the yelling with noise and sugar.

By the time Meg comes in, she is calm, at least outwardly. But her eyes look red around the edges. She gets down on the floor with both boys to give them squeezes. She hugs them until they wriggle away, laughing.

"Well," she says, sweeping her hair up into a knot on top of her head, "it looks like we're on our own tonight, but I think we still owe ourselves an adventure. What do you say, Ellie?" We exchange a look over the top of the boys' heads.

"I may have an idea," I say, and she smiles.

◇ ◇ ◇

We don't get back from Bill and Will's Putt-Putt Emporium, the miniature golf course that Bert's brothers built, until after dark. Meg has to carry a sleeping Finn into the house. I help Patrick find his pajamas and put bubble-mint toothpaste on his toothbrush.

"Thanks for your help today," Meg whispers when she steps out of the living room, where the boys are sleeping on cots. There isn't enough space in the trailer for them to have an actual room. We're calling it "indoor camping," and they love it.

"No problem," I say, even as I wonder how often Dad is the guy I saw earlier today, temperamental and unhelpful like a too-tired kid. Actually, strike that. The boys were more adult than he was. They didn't complain about the change of plans or even ask why their dad didn't come golfing with us. Maybe they're used to it. I really, really hope that's not true.

Meg yanks out her ponytail and leans against the wall in the hallway. "He's not always like this," she replies, like she is reading my thoughts.

"'There's a whole lot of wiggle room between always and never,'" I say, quoting Mema.

Meg sighs. "You know what? You're right. I'm done defending him. His behavior today was unacceptable. I'm sorry you had to see it." She puts a hand on my shoulder. For once I don't mind. "But I hope you get to see some of the good things about him too." Meg might wear scrunchies and spend an inordinate amount of time on Pinterest, but she's tougher than she looks. Right now, I like her a million times more than Dad.

I am exhausted, and my stomach roils from one too many corn dogs at the Putt-Putt Emporium, but instead of going to bed when Meg disappears to take a shower, I roll out to the porch. I sit in the dark for a long time, watching the light from the garage flicker as Dad works. I've done the math. They've got nine days left. How can you prove you're a good person in less than two weeks? Dad's great at deadlines, but I don't think he's going to make this one.

14

Q and A

The deli counter at Food & Co. is hoppin' on a Friday afternoon. Everybody planning their weekend picnics, I suppose.

"Mrs. Jenkins, your order's up!" Bert calls from behind the glass counter. Seeing him in his plastic hairnet is the sole reason I suggested this location for our pageant rehearsal. That and the free samples.

Mrs. Jenkins powers up her motorized shopping cart and scoots alongside me.

"Hello, dear," she says. When she holds up her hand for the pound of Swiss, her arm jiggles. It makes me miss Mema.

"Bert, focus!" Coralee barks from the stool beside the

spicy pickle display. She's one to talk. I saw her sneak some taffy from the barrels by the register when Mr. Akers, Bert's dad, wasn't looking. Coralee in a room full of snacks is a distracted Coralee.

"Multitasking is a false supposition," he says, slicing a log of salami into thin rounds. "The human brain is incapable of doing two things simultaneously. But it *can* switch back and forth at varying rates of speed." He hands the paper-wrapped meat to a woman on a cell phone with a baby strapped to her front. "My speed just happens to be faster than most."

Coralee starts picking taffy out of her teeth.

"Attractive," I say, and she pretends to flick whatever she found at me.

"You're up next anyway." She points her wet finger at me. "Bert, throw Ellie a question!"

We are practicing for the first stage of the pageant— the interview round. And what better place to answer potentially deep personal questions than the middle of the meat section?

"All right. Miss Ellie Cowan, if you were stuck on a desert island, what one item would you take with you?" he asks.

"That *cannot* be a real question," I say.

"Truly, it is," Coralee sings, and spins on her stool.

I throw up my hands. "What's next—if you were a color, what would it be and why?"

Coralee tilts her head. "That's actually not a bad one."

Bert clears his throat to get us back on track.

"Okay, okay! If I were stuck on a desert island . . ." I look around the store. Jars of pigs' feet floating in clear liquid sit next to plastic-wrapped pecan sandies. Paperback romances and hand soap line the aisle behind me. Baskets filled with homemade bread and cinnamon rolls sit in the front window next to the post office station, where you can send packages. Food & Co. is an island unto itself. Maybe I should just say that. "Ummm—"

"Don't say 'um,'" Bert interrupts. "No 'ums,' 'likes,' 'uhs.' They make you sound unsure and uncouth."

"I bet your girlfriend would never say 'um.'" That was a cheap shot, but I am not "uncouth." Bert is enjoying *managing* us a little too much if you ask me.

Bert drops a turkey loaf onto the floor. "Who?"

"Maaaaaya," Coralee drawls.

His ears turn beet red. "Maya is not my girlfriend. We connect on an intellectual level."

"Whatever you need to tell yourself," I say, and then we both make kissy faces at him until he points a pair of tongs at me and orders me to answer.

"Fine. I'd probably take my favorite cast-iron skillet."

"For real?" Coralee asks.

"Yes, *for real*. How else am I going to fry up all the insects and octopuses I'm going to catch?" I try not to think about the fact that Dad was the one who gave me the skillet. If I'm on a desert island, I can't afford to toss one of my few means of survival, even if it came from a disreputable source.

Coralee tilts her head. "Octopuses? That can't be right."

"Actually, according to Merriam-Webster, either 'octopuses' or 'octopi' is correct," Bert clarifies. "But chances of catching one are slim unless you use a spear . . . ," he pauses, cradling a hunk of ham in his arms, "or trawling pot."

Coralee and I both stare at Bert as he feeds the ham into the whirring deli slicer. If anyone could survive on a desert island, it would be him. I shake my head.

"Whatever. Y'all stop mocking my answer. What would *you* take, Coralee?"

"Easy. I'd bring Francis," she says, flicking the jar of pigs' feet with her finger so they slosh in their juices.

"The cockatoo?" I ask.

She shrugs. "He'd get lonesome without me."

After practice, Coralee and I head to the center of town to wait by the fountain for Bert to get off his shift. Will of Bill and Will's Putt-Putt Emporium is picking us up and taking us to our final rehearsal at the Rocking Horse before the pageant next week.

A girl with long red hair and a fiddle sits on the edge of the fountain with her case open on the ground in front of her. She plays a country tune I can't name, and her long, gauzy skirt sways in the breeze.

Coralee stretches herself out along the fountain's opposite edge like a mermaid in the sun.

"So, what song are you going to sing for your talent?"

"Don't know," she answers with her eyes closed. "Dolly's always my muse of choice, but everybody's doing Dolly nowadays, so I might switch it up."

I lean over and dip my fingers in the cool water. My reflection turns wavy.

"How about you? You gonna bake something?"

"Yeah. Of course. But it's not like in speech class, with the snowball cookies. Nobody wants to watch me roll balls of dough. I've got to come up with something spectacular." I've been thinking about it a lot. I'm surprised by how much I care. But it's not about winning the pageant. It's about showing the judges that I am more than what they see. I may not be able to answer their questions like a beauty queen, but baking is a language I can speak.

Across from us, the fiddler switches tunes. Coralee sits

up in delight. "Ohhh, Elton John." She slips off her shoes and jumps into the fountain. "I'm down with that." Then, for all of Eufaula to see, Coralee dances in the water to the beat.

She sways and spins and tips her head back with her eyes closed and a satisfied grin. The glitter in her orange crop top sparkles. She lifts her arms over her head to pirouette. It's better than a ballet. Better than a pageant. It's Coralee at her finest. She was made for music the way I'm made for baking—we both can hear the secrets whispered through our craft and we know how to make those secrets work for us.

It's why Coralee is *already* a triple threat and a star in my book—with or without the Little Miss sash over her shoulder. I pick up her camera and take a few shots. Coralee's got her own kind of deep magic. But she's determined not to see it until a committee tells her it's true.

The fiddler bobs her head in approval of Coralee's water dance and plays the song through twice. When it's over, a few passersby clap and throw bills into the fiddler's case. Coralee bows. It's a smashing hit until a police officer checking parking meters barks at her to get out.

True to form, she grunts and lurches her way to the edge and then climbs back over like a drowned zombie until the officer rolls his eyes and zooms away.

"Nice," I say, and she flicks me with her wet hair.

We watch the fiddler pack up her case. "The song she was playing was 'Tiny Dancer,'" Coralee says, and then she adds in a smaller voice, "It's my mom's favorite."

I keep my eyes on the water dripping from her bare toes, because we don't do emotion all that well, "Well then, I think you've found your song."

15

Smells Like Tween Spirit

The green Food & Co. van screeches to a halt in front of the town square half an hour after the fiddler's departure. Will Akers throws open the sliding door and shouts, "Your chariot awaits!" Then he checks his watch. "But hustle up. I've got to be back at the Emporium by five."

"Our knight in shining armor," Coralee croons as Will, who is home from college for the summer, loads my wheelchair in the back while Bert barks directions up front. She's kidding, but Will *definitely* has a good thing going for him. With his late afternoon stubble and his wrinkled beach T-shirt, he's a taller, less polished version of Bert. I dig it. Which is why I'm basically mute whenever he's around.

When Bert tries to ask me more interview questions on the ride over, I shake my head and act like I can't hear him over the wind pouring in the open windows. Coralee is too busy watching the town fly by and humming "Tiny Dancer" to notice my silence. I stare at the back of Will's neck, where two freckles almost touch. His dark hair swirls around in the breeze.

When Will drops us off in front of the Rocking Horse with a too-quick wave goodbye, it takes no time at all for my nerves to transfer from him to rehearsal. As I roll past the still-leaking water fountain, part of me hopes Rae Ann was unable to locate a suitable ramp. For once, inaccessibility could work in my favor.

But there it is, *front and center* when I get into the auditorium, an extra-long ramp that reaches almost to the round tables in order to make up for the height of the stage. Rae Ann has rented me an airplane runway. Awesome.

"Girls!" she cries from the back row of seats, making me jump. Lady's got some lurking skills. "I was just taking in the lay of the land. Isn't this stage just *perfection* for our big show next week?" She gets up and sashays over to us with her arms open wide. Today she wears a purple velvet jumpsuit that is very tight across her lower half. I'd bet all my seventy-five-dollar registration fee that it says LITTLE

MISS '86 in rhinestones on the back. But I'm not checking to see.

Maya sits cross-legged on the stage with a book in her lap, but she looks up and waves when we come down the aisle. The rest of the girls are already up there too. So it's just me and Coralee at the base of the ramp. I take what I hope is a very subtle deep breath and roll to the edge. Coralee steps on it and jumps a couple of times, testing its sturdiness for me. When it doesn't move, she nods. I reverse a foot and then take it in one smooth push. My chair goes up easy and before I know it, I'm on the stage, facing rows and rows of empty seats. I want to throw up now more than ever.

"Okay, ladies!" Rae Ann calls. "I hope you're all stretched and loose, because it is time to get a *move* on it!"

"I thought this was just a song," I hiss at Coralee. "You *promised*, no dancing!"

"I didn't *know*," she whispers back. We both shoot Bert death stares at his spot in the front row. As our manager, it was his job to warn us about things like this.

"I know we don't usually do a choreographed dance with the Little Miss anthem," Rae Ann says now, and Bert points his favorite Bic at her by way of explanation, "but I thought it might be fun to shake things up a bit this year." She shimmies her shoulders. "We want to give the people a pageant they will *never* forget. Show them what our Little Miss Boots and Bows girls can do!"

That's it. I'm out of here. I did not sign up for this. I begin to roll toward the edge of the stage, but before I can get my wheels on the ramp, Rae Ann reaches out one lavender-tipped fingernail and taps my shoulder. Then she leans down and whispers, "Don't you worry, little Miss Ellie. I have the perfect solution worked out for you." Every nerve in my body goes on high alert.

Rae Ann raises her voice again to ballpark volume. "I've marked off a circle in the center of the stage. Ellie, I want you on this X right here, right in the middle. The rest of you will take your places along the perimeter."

I roll to the X marked in blue tape and turn back around. Rae Ann has put me in the dead center of the bull's-eye. I dart a nervous glance at Coralee, but she's not looking at me. She's frowning at her position on the outer circle.

When we're all in place, Rae Ann scurries to the side of the stage, where a CD player sits in the wings. I didn't even know CD players still existed. She walks back to us, cradling it in her arms like a baby.

"Now, when I press play, I want you girls in the outer circle to shimmy clockwise, so go right. And Ellie, I want you to shimmy counterclockwise to your left, okay?

We'll begin the song on the second beat. Got it?"

No, I don't "got it." But Rae Ann doesn't allow any time for objections. She hits play and orchestral music crackles from the tiny speakers at a volume determined to burst my eardrums. Immediately, all nine girls along the outer circle begin to walk around me.

"Always face the audience, ladies! Rae Ann shouts, and Maya and one of the blond ones whose name I can never remember turn to face the seats. "Ellie, move, darlin'. Shimmy to the left!" Panicked at being yelled at by this tiny woman, I start to wheel myself in the opposite direction of everybody else. How does she expect me to face the audience? It's not like I can "shimmy" my wheels sideways. And I don't even know how fast or slow she wants me to go! I forget to sing the words altogether until we hit "eternal flame of our light." But I guess whatever we do is good enough, because Rae Ann claps so hard she jangles a gold bangle all the way off her wrist.

"That was just . . . That was beautiful, ladies," she says, her voice breaking at the end. Whoa, take it down a notch, lady. It's not like we're at the Tonys.

She walks toward the stage with her hands clasped under her chin, and her gaze skims over every contestant until it lands smack-dab on me. So it is only me she's looking at when she says, "I couldn't ask for anything more for our Little Miss Pageant." This time I can't hide the shiver that snakes up my spine.

After we pack up our stuff, I am more than ready to escape into the June heat. But Bert lingers by the glass doors, talking to Maya about spelling bee stuff. I turn to Coralee, ready to vent.

"Can you believe that dance or walk or *shimmy* or whatever? I mean, what even *was* that?"

"Yep. Pretty unbelievable," she mumbles.

"We should get Bert to check the 'Rules and Regulations'"—I toss up some heavy air quotes—"to see if it's even allowed," but she doesn't laugh. "Wouldn't you just love to see her get schooled by a thirteen-year-old boy?"

Still nothing. It's not like Coralee had to spin like a hubcap in the center of a circle of dancing girls for the last hour. She should be the one trying to cheer *me* up. Not the other way around. What's *with* her?

16

Friends in Low Places

I have the whole ride to try to guess what happened that has Coralee at a loss for words. But by the time Will drops us off in front of my trailer, I'm still no closer to figuring it out and it's making me squirmy, like when there's a fly in the room you can hear but can't see. I did everything she asked. I entered the pageant. I didn't quit when Rae Ann pulled out the world's worst ramp. I found a dress. I practiced my desert island answers. I even did the song and dance! So why does it feel like she's mad at me? I could ignore it. I *should* ignore it. Coralee's got more moods than the sky has stars. But the not-knowing's got me itchy with worry.

"Hey." I grab Coralee's elbow before she can dart away

between the holly trees that separate her trailer from mine. "Is, uh, something wrong?" She barely glances at me. I feel like Finn, tugging at Patrick's shirt when his brother won't play with him. I let go.

"Nope. I'm good," she says in the flat voice she uses on Sierra at school. How could she use that voice on *me*?

I turn to go in, but then add, "Yeah, you sound *good*." The words are so quiet, I'm not even sure she heard until I hear behind me, "What?"

I spin back around. Coralee's got her arms crossed. "What do you want from me? Do you really need me to stand here and listen to you complain about the pageant *again*? And then thank you *again* for doing it for me?"

"What? *No*."

"Good. Because I think if you hate it so much, maybe you *should* just drop out."

Maybe I should . . . *what?* I search her face for the joke, but her mouth is stretched in a thin line and she won't look at me. I'm disoriented, like when my old physical therapist used to let go while I was standing and I'd have to remember how to stay upright on my own two feet.

"Whatever," I say. My voice cracks, giving me away, if she took the time to notice. Which she doesn't. I don't understand what's happening or how I'm supposed to fix it or if it's even my job to fix it. Why is she being like this? I try

141

to take a breath like Mema always tells me to do when I get worked up, but the air in my lungs feels too thin and tight.

Coralee moves toward the trees, but then turns back at the last minute. My body eases. She's going to say she's sorry. This is what we do. We yell at each other and then we make up—"easy peasy," as she would say. I'm already opening my mouth to accept her apology, but what she says instead is, "Listen, do what you want, but I think maybe we should rehearse separately from now on."

Then she's gone, and there's no one but the crickets to hear me whisper, "Yeah. Fine."

Flour. Yeast. Salt. Butter. Sugar. Eggs.

You should be able to make almost anything out of that. Except today, I can't. The kitchen cabinets drip with splattered egg yolk. The stove is dusted with flour that exploded out of the mixer. The yeast didn't bubble in the warm water. My cardamom cinnamon rolls didn't rise. The butter burned on the stove. And somehow I have brown sugar hardening in my ponytail. Basically, everything that could go wrong, did.

I lean my head against the edge of the counter. None of this mess is turning into the showstopper that will win the talent portion of the pageant. And none of it is distracting me from the fact that it's been three days since

I've spoken to Coralee. The hurt hasn't gotten less. If anything it's started to throb worse, like a hangnail I can't stop picking. That's the problem. How am I supposed to create a masterpiece worthy of first place when all I can think about is my stupid friend and her stupid attitude about a stupid pageant?

I lift my head and start throwing wads of hard, flat, lumpy cinnamon roll into the trash. It feels good. Mad is better than sad. Mad is *motivation*. I scrub an angry tear off my cheek with the back of my hand. I'll start fresh, and whatever comes out will be ten million times more dramatic and win-worthy than a pan of old dough. Three days ago I didn't even want to win Little Miss anything. But *now* I do. Because now I have to beat Coralee. I hurl the crusty pan into the sink. She'll see she can't just boss me around and then forget about me when I don't behave like she wants me to. I *need* this.

"Dad!" I shout through the kitchen window. He looks up from his spot at the card table in the garage. "You have to take me to Mema's!" It's not a question.

"Hiya," I say, surprised that Grandpa is opening the door. Today his hair is brushed and combed neatly to the side. His green plaid shirt is washed and ironed. There's a toothpick parked in the corner of his mouth just like the old days, when he was doing his woodworking. When he smiles, his eyes twinkle with mischief.

"Marianne, those door-to-door pest control people are back!" he shouts back down the hallway.

"What?" Mema yells from somewhere inside. "You tell them that I'm calling the police! That is criminal behavior! There is no soliciting in our dang neighborhood! They are harassing the elderly! They know—" Her head pops up over Grandpa's shoulder. "Oh."

I give her a little wave.

She swats him with the dish towel. "Jonah, don't be messin' with me. I was ready to hunt down the pepper spray."

He takes the toothpick out of his mouth and points it at her. "Got to keep you on your toes."

"Job well done. Now back up, old man, and let our granddaughter in here before she melts."

I follow them down the hallway to the kitchen, where a pot of vegetable soup simmers on the stove and cornbread muffins cool their round golden tops in a pan on the counter. Clearly Mema's not suffering my cooking curse today.

"You stayin' for lunch?" she asks.

"If you'll have me."

"Always," she says.

Grandpa taps the gray garment bag on my lap.

"What you got there, my girl?"

"Well, I was hoping Mema could help me with something." I take a deep breath, unzip the bag, and unveil my blue-and-white dress. "Do you have time to take in the sides of this, just a little?"

She gathers the dress from me and turns it inside out to inspect it. "Looks like it'd be pretty easy to unpick the seam right around the zipper. Shouldn't take much. Come back to the bedroom and we'll have a look."

Finally, *one* thing's going right today.

"Jonah, don't you touch that soup until I get back," she calls. "It's got to simmer!"

"I ain't touching nothing, woman! I'm going to work my puzzle!" he shouts back. After living away from them for a year, I forgot how much of their conversation is yelling. I missed it.

"He still doing the crossword?" I ask after Mema shuts the door and I slip the dress on over my head.

"Yep. Dr. Hirschman actually wrote it on a prescription slip for him. Your grandfather got such a kick out of it, he taped it to the fridge."

"Does it help?"

She shrugs. "Doesn't hurt. Now, sit still so I don't poke you with my pins."

I'm barely breathing as she pinches the fabric between her fingers and quickly slips the straight pins along the side of the dress under my arm.

"Now," she says as she works, "does this project have anything to do with the seventy-five dollars you borrowed from me?"

"I'm sorry I haven't paid you back yet."

She secures the pin she's holding and then waves her hands.

"I wasn't fishin', Ellie. And you didn't answer my question."

I sigh and then wince as one of the pins nicks me in the rib.

"Take that thing off before you bleed all over it. I'm done." She helps me get it over my head and then moves to the sewing machine. "We can talk while I work."

The *one* time I wish the sewing machine were louder. "Yeah, it's for a project."

"The favor for a friend, right?"

I squirm in my chair. "Right. Except, it's not so much for my friend now. And she's not so much my friend, I guess."

Mema pauses her pedal and the needle slows to a stop. She turns fully around to face me, and I recognize the look. It's the "porch talk" look.

146

"Honey, I have been around a long time. Long enough that decades feel like minutes. I swear every time I turn around it's breakfast again. Now don't laugh, because I'm not kidding and what I'm about to say is no joke."

I lose the smile and settle in for the speech I know is coming.

She points a finger at me. "Here's a thing I learned over the course of all these years: you only get one or two really good friends in a lifetime. I mean the kind that stick around through thick and thin and fightin' and fun. One or two. Three, if you're lucky. That's *it*."

Porch talk over, Mema turns back to the sewing machine. My heart pinches worse than the pinpricks. I guess Coralee wasn't a lifer kind of friend. I thought she was. I really did. But *unlike her*, I can admit when I'm wrong.

"Yeah. So?" I say, picking at Mema because I've been itching for a satisfying argument ever since Coralee disappeared behind the holly trees.

"So," she says with her back to me, "you better hang on to the ones you got."

17

Please Hold Your Applause

Dear Ellie,

Greetings from Texola, our last stop on the Route 66 tour! Remember that toast at J&P's Diner back in Nashville? The one next to the children's hospital? Remember what number ten on the menu was? The Holy Roller—with eggs, hash browns, and a side of toast with Jesus's face on it. You loved it! Well, the Tumbleweed Grill & Country Store here in Texola serves Route 66 toast! Every piece has that 66 road sign burned right into the center. It's almost as good as J&P's, but you can't really compete with

Jesus toast, can you? I'm attaching a picture.

Texola feels like an empty set from a Wild West show. The windows in the deserted buildings are broken. Weeds poke up through the pavement at the abandoned gas station. The only sounds are wind and the occasional blue jay. It's spooky, but cool. We plan to cross the state line so we can stick our toes into Texas and then turn around and speed right back to you!

Two sleeps until we are reunited! Beau Jr. is counting down the seconds.

Love you, baby,

Mom

When Susie pulls the Caddy alongside my trailer to drive us to the first official round of the pageant on Friday morning, I let out a little whoosh of air. It's one-half relief, one-half dread. Honestly? I wasn't sure Coralee would show. I wouldn't put it past her to order Susie to zoom on by me in a cloud of dust. But now that she's here, I don't know how we're going to fill the miles and minutes of awkwardness. Here's hoping Bert acts as a decent buffer.

Coralee doesn't so much as look at me while Bert

hustles to get my chair in the trunk. She just sits there with her nose turned up, wearing the mint-green skirt with the black fringe and matching top that *I* found for her at Timeless Treasures. We are already late. But I make sure to take my sweet time buckling my seat belt. I have been practicing my speaking voice and my smile, and I'm not ready to let Coralee make me quit just yet.

Susie blares Bonnie Raitt and taps her unlit cigarette on the steering wheel to the rhythm. We keep the windows up. I stare at the back of Coralee's head, but she doesn't turn once all the way there. Before I can shove it down, hurt wells up like a burp. I swallow hard and focus on what's ahead. It's Round One. I should be nervous. But I'm not. At least not yet. I've been too focused on coexisting with Coralee for the next several hours. I should thank her for the distraction. See how she likes that.

When we arrive at the Rocking Horse, the glass on the ticket booth has been washed and the gold handles on the doors polished. Inside, the stale candy and popcorn at the concession stand have been replaced with Little Miss Boots and Bows T-shirts and bandanas. You can even order a personalized photo . . . for twenty-five dollars plus tax.

A little girl in a tight gold sequined dress stands by the red velvet ropes. Her hair is sprayed high and stiff, just like Rae Ann's. She gives us a smile with four baby teeth missing. It's like looking at a forty-year-old woman trapped in a child's body. When she hands me a printed program, I stare at it so as not to stare at her.

The program is a dozen or so glossy pages. I thumb through it to delay going up onstage. The first half tells the history of the Little Miss Boots and Bows Pageant, which Rae Ann recited on our very first day, and the second half lists the profiles of the most recent Little Miss winners from Oklahoma and the current contestants. When I get to the very last page, I jerk to a halt in the middle of the aisle. Bert runs into me with an *oof*. There's my picture in full color, along with Coralee's and Maya's and the rest of the girls.

We all had to turn in a photo along with our registration, and I am just now figuring out why. In Coralee's, her hair is teased high up on her forehead. Her lips glisten with cherry-red gloss. And her blue eyes look as big as saucers. I remember helping her attach those false eyelashes, right before she went off to get her "professional headshot" done at the mall. I, however, sent in my class picture from school. In it, my eyes are half-closed and my mouth half-open. The school photographer had brought puppets, *puppets* to get us to smile. I was in the middle of telling him exactly what I thought about that. I didn't know I'd have to see it blown up to *half the page*. Yet another detail Coralee forgot to mention.

151

I'm about to turn to Bert to complain about my photo op when the lights dim and Rae Ann herself sticks her head out from behind the curtain to hurry us down the aisle. About a third of the rows are filled. Judging by all the phones held up to face the stage, I'm guessing it's the families of the contestants. Either that or a whole lot of people who are about to be confused as to why their showing of *To Kill a Mockingbird* took such a strange turn.

Up in front of the stage, all the tables but one have been removed. At the lonely table in the center, two women and a man sit behind a desk lamp with note cards in front of them. I guess those are the judges. They look half-asleep.

"Goodness, you two are likely to give me a heart attack," Rae Ann whispers to me and Coralee once we are assembled backstage. She tugs on a heavy jeweled necklace at her throat. The blue gems are as big as dice. "For the talent round, I expect you not to cut it so close. Timeliness is next to godliness, you know."

"I thought it was cleanliness that's next to godliness," I say, but Rae Ann is already turning away to call the other girls to the stage for our big anthem. I forget for a second that we're in a fight and look to Coralee to roll my eyes over the ridiculousness that is Rae Ann Perkins, but she has already left to join the rest of the girls. The surprise of her absence makes my vision go watery. I squint so I won't cry. I'm alone in the dark on the edge of a stage in a theater where I am about to participate in my first and last ever pageant. I just want my best friend.

When the stage lights hit Rae Ann, she cranks up her smile to megawattage like a windup toy come to life. "All right, my fine folks," she begins. "Are you ready for the ninety-ninth Little Miss Boots and Bows Pageant?" A few people clap. Not enough to satisfy Rae Ann, who turns it up a notch.

"Now, while I haven't been around for them all"— she pauses to wink her big fake eyelashes, which gets a laugh—"I can assure you this one will be our best pageant yet! We have girls from all backgrounds bringing their beauty and talent from across the great state of Oklahoma. Now"—another long pause as she scans the crowd—"let me ask you again . . . are you ready for the ninety-ninth Little Miss Boots and Bows Pageant?"

This time the crowd erupts in cheers and even a few whistles. It's terrifying. Rae Ann smiles, and my stomach bottoms out as she signals us onstage.

We take our places along the blue tape, me in the center of the world's worst merry-go-round. I stare at my knees so I don't have to see the faces looking at me. The music blasts on before I'm ready, and the rest of the girls start moving. After a split second, when my arms refuse to listen to my brain, I begin to roll in the opposite direction. Coralee turns her head toward the crowd and away from me at every pass. I mouth the words to the song. No one can tell. In my head, I sing a new version instead:

"When I wish upon a dream,
   (When I show up on this scene,)
I can see the world, it seems,
   (I can see these beauty queens,)
In the distance shining bright
   (In the spotlight smiling bright)
With our eternal flame of light.
   (With their eternal teeth so white.)

Little Misses shine our light,
   (Little Misses shine your light,)
Share the love with all our might
   (Show your teeth with all your might)
Until the world in beauty unites.
   (Until the world in Crest unites.)
We can share the love,
   (We can share the toothpaste,)
We can share the love
   (We can share the toothpaste)

Little Misses,
   (Little Misses,)
We can share the *love*."
   (We can share the *tooooooothpaaaassste*.)

Once the song is over and I am safely offstage and hiding in the wings again, I have only a second to wish Maya luck. She's first up for the interview round and doesn't seem nervous at all as she walks onstage in a yellow jumpsuit and black flats. She said she needed this pageant to prepare for the pressure of the spelling bee, but she seems the chillest of us all. I roll over to the edge of the curtain to watch.

Maya gets the perfect question: "If you could pick three words to describe yourself, what would they be?" I can't even *begin* to spell, much less define, the three words she lists. And I know I'm not the only one, because even though they're trying to be subtle about it, two of the three judges are clearly googling the definitions on their phones. Behind them, Bert smiles from the front row. Her question over, Maya exits the stage with a graceful wave.

Two more contestants go: "What's your favorite flower and why?" and "How can we as a state better educate our children?" Then it's Coralee's turn. As she walks onstage, I order myself *not* to care.

"Miss Coralee," Rae Ann says, "could you please tell the judges what your definition of success is." Coralee steps up to the microphone. Her hair shines in the spotlight, and the black tassels on her skirt sway as she clasps her hands together in front of her.

"Success to me is doing everything in my power to pursue my dream of becoming world-famous for my acting, dancing, and most especially"—she gives the judges a wink—"my singing talents. Through these three things I hope to bring entertainment and also joy to people out there who might need a distraction from their day-to-day lives. Hopefully"—she pauses for dramatic effect—"if I do it right, I can bring a smile to *anyone's* face." Then she beams a perfect, Crest-worthy smile.

The judges bend their heads over their scorecards. When a few people clap, Rae Ann reminds them to hold their applause until the end. Wow, Coralee was so *smooth*. I am so not ready for this. I can't. I can't do it. I need Coralee to tell me I can do anything, because we are super women and awesome and will basically be running the country in a few short years. But I don't have Coralee. I only have the voice in my head screaming, *This will be a disaster!*

I begin reversing into the safety of the stage curtains when Rae Ann calls "Miss Ellie Cowan" to the stage. All the blood drains from my head. I think I might pass out.

The Cowan Family Lotto lucky ball number nine is *Imagine your favorite place*. I close my eyes and think, *Anywhere but here*, then roll myself onstage with shaking arms.

The spotlight is blazing hot. My black T-shirt and black skirt, the closest thing I will ever get to snappy casual, draws the heat like a solar panel and I am immediately sweating. But Rae Ann doesn't give me even a second to compose myself before she says, "We here at the Boots and Bows Pageant pride ourselves on crowning poised, proud, and yes, pretty"—she titters—"winners as role models for our future Little Misses. So please tell us, Ellie, who is the biggest role model in *your* life?"

My mind goes blank. Bert asked me what I would take to a desert island, which celebrity I would eat dinner with, what quality I like most about myself. But he never asked me this. The only way off this stage is to answer. Somehow I manage to roll toward the microphone where Coralee stood not two minutes ago. Of *course* it's too high. I reach up to lower it, hoping the black T-shirt hides the dampness under my arms. But before I can get to it, Rae Ann is at my side, saying, "Here, let me!" a little too loudly and removing the mic from its stand. Except instead of handing it to me, she crouches down and holds it, like I am five years old. Her face is inches from mine. Caked-on foundation paints lines in the cracks of her neck.

"Umm." Oh great, I'm off to a stellar start. "If I had to pick my biggest role model, I would, uh . . ." If Mom were here she'd know what to do. She'd get me the heck off this stage, for one thing. But she *isn't* here. I'm going to have to dig my way out of this one myself. "Uh, so, my mom rode a horse named Sparky a couple of weeks ago." Why am I talking about *horses*? "I, uh, know that doesn't sound like a big deal. But my mom is kind of terrified of big animals. I mean *terrified*. We used to live in Nashville, and she would turn her head away from the farms as we passed, in case a cow gave her the side-eye. But just last week, she met a bull named Beauregard. You see—" I stop. Now bulls? What am I *doing*? I try to swallow, but my throat is itchy and dry and there's not enough spit in my mouth to do any good. *Get yourself back on track, Ellie.*

"This summer she got married to my gym teacher, Hutch, and they're off on their honeymoon. It's the longest she's left me since, well, ever. But it's good," I say more to myself than for them, "because it means she's doing new things like riding horses and meeting bulls. She's spent most of my life doing mom stuff, so it's about time she has some adventures. She's always been my biggest advocate, fighting with insurance and schools and hospitals to make sure I get the best care. But I've learned to do a lot of that myself, mostly because she showed me how. So now she can do more stuff on her own. And . . . I guess I can too."

I blink down at my hands, white-knuckled where they grip my wheels. Talking about Mom has made me miss her more than ever. I'm tired of all these people staring at me and the heat of the spotlight. If I were really my own advocate, I'd get off this stage and never come back.

"So that's it. That's my answer." I turn to Rae Ann and push the mic out of my face. "My mom is my role model."

I'm already backing up, ready to roll toward the safety and darkness backstage, when Rae Ann throws one sinewy arm around me and traps me in place. Then she turns to the audience and whispers into the mic, "Wasn't that just beautiful, everybody?"

The auditorium bursts into applause and I jump. When Rae Ann releases me to wipe an invisible tear from her eye, I race out of the spotlight, past Coralee and Maya and the rest of the girls watching in the wings. And then I sit in a corner by myself, my heart racing, until I am sure everyone has gone.

18

Model Behavior

In the half-inch of space where the curtain almost meets the wall, I wait for the theater lights to grow brighter so everyone can make their way out. And then I watch them dim again in preparation for tonight's film. It is dark and cool back here in my corner of the stage. The heavy velvet curtain muffles all sounds. It's soothing, like being underwater.

But I can't hide back here forever. Bert has to be wondering where I am. And Coralee's my ride. I try not to think too hard about the fact that my once best friend is now just an Uber. I breathe out a heavy sigh. This day has been one long emotional thunderstorm, and I just want out. I begin to roll toward the ramp, but I'm not even halfway out when the sound of Rae Ann's husky voice stops me. I duck back behind the curtain and peer out. Her back is to me. She's facing a dark-haired woman with glasses. A worn leather satchel that Bert would die for is slung across her shoulder. The woman holds a tape recorder in front of Rae Ann's face. She looks bored. But Rae Ann doesn't seem to notice.

"I could not be more proud of our girls this year! The pageant is shaping up to be the best one yet!" she exclaims at full volume.

The woman winces and pulls the tape recorder back a few inches. I see her glance at her watch. She's as ready as I am to get out of here.

"So you don't think the era of pageants and prom kings and queens is over?"

Ooh, this is gonna be good. I scoot out a little more so I can see Rae Ann's face. She purses her lips so hard they practically disappear.

"I do *not*. Our focus on scholarship, inclusion, and unity is timeless. These girls work their behinds off to show the very best side of themselves, and I don't see what's wrong with celebrating the beauty in each of them."

"Yes, but beauty on what terms?" the reporter asks. "Who gets to decide what is beautiful and what isn't? Societal ideals of beauty are evolving."

Rae Ann sniffs. "The Little Miss Boots and Bows

Pageant is not above changing with the times. The past several years we have had quite a diverse cast of participants competing for the crown." She leans forward, her lips centimeters from the tape recorder. "Did you see that little girl today? The one who said her mother was her role model?"

My skin prickles as a chill washes over me. That's me. Rae Ann is talking about *me*. I need to get out before I can hear any more, but she is right in front of the ramp! She's blocking my only exit. I rock back and forth, trapped.

"That little girl"—Rae Ann pauses—"is *my* role model. She might be wheelchair-bound, but she gets up there on that stage and works just as hard as the rest of them. That's true beauty, right there." She taps the top of the tape recorder with the tip of a manicured nail. "You want to write about the pageant. Put *that* in your article or your blog or whatever this is for."

Wheelchair-*bound*? Is she *kidding* me? Like my chair is some torture device instead of the means of freedom that lets me navigate my *entire life*?

They begin to walk up the aisle. Rae Ann is still talking, but I can't listen to another word. I back into my corner, cover my ears, and rest my head on my knees.

When I am 100 percent sure they're gone, I coast down the ramp, but then slow my roll. I can't face my friends yet. I feel wrecked. I'm not sure I can handle anyone right now. But as I leave the auditorium and roll down the hall toward the lobby, I spy a pair of long brown legs in my path, breaking up the ugly pattern of paisley carpet. I swerve and then stop.

"Hey, Maya." She looks up from her book. "Why are you sitting here?"

She sighs. "Today was too easy. This isn't helping me prepare for the Bee at all." She slams her book closed without even saving her place. "Quick, ask me the hardest word you can think of and I'll tell you how to spell it."

"For real?"

"Yes, for real. Life is a test, Ellie."

"O-kay," I say to buy some time, because my head is still full of Rae Ann, and all the words I can think of right now sound like something out of a Dr. Seuss book. Cat. Hat. Cat. Mat. "Ummm, spell the word from *Mary Poppins*. Supercali—*you* know."

She sighs like I am a toddler asking for a second juice cup. "Really? That's your big word?"

I move past her and call over my shoulder, "Well, if you can't do it . . ."

Maya stands up. "No. Of course I can do it! I just figured you would pick a word that was actually, you know, in the dictionary." She crosses her arms. "S-u-o-i-c-o-d-i-l-a-i-p-x-e-c-i-t-s-i-l-i-g-a-r-f-i-l-a-c-r-e-p-u-s."

I squint while I whisper it back to myself. "No way that's right."

She sits back down. Opens her book. "I spelled it backward."

"Of course you did." Maya might be tied with Coralee for most determined. "So?"

"So what?"

I roll back until I am right next to her and can lean my head against the wall. "Why are you still here?" I want to know, and also, the more I talk to her, the longer I can delay going outside and telling Bert and Coralee what happened.

She leans her head back on the wall like me, so we are mirror images of tiredness. "My dad had to work and my mom's in class."

"Class?"

"She's getting her bachelor's in social work. She'll be the first person in her family to get a degree." She waves her bookmark at me. It's a bus receipt. "I'm happy to wait and take the bus." I know she means it, but I can also tell that she'd rather her mom could come get her. She says *I'm happy* like I write *I'm great* to Mom in every one of my emails. We want our moms to achieve their dreams. But we also want them to be there for our dreams.

Maya should win this pageant. She's the most talented

one of us, I think. And then I immediately feel like a traitor to Coralee, even though I don't owe her a thing right now. And then that gets me back to thinking about my no-good day, and I get bone-tired all over again.

"Well, see you tomorrow. Rounds two and three, here we go!" I say with a smile, but it must be my bit-my-tongue smile, because Maya frowns.

"Hey, Ellie," she says as I start to roll away. "You know how I said life is a test?"

"Yeah?"

"My mom told me that. She says it all the time. But there's a second part. She says, 'Life is a test. Make sure you take it on your own terms.'" Did Maya hear what Rae Ann told the reporter? Is she feeling sorry for me? Is *this* a test? But before I can ask her, she goes back to reading her book.

It should be night when I exit the Rocking Horse Theater. Surely I've been in here hours, years even, waiting for the echo of Rae Ann's words to fade? But the sun hangs like a bully in the sky and the sludgy smell of hot asphalt stings my nose. Bert and Coralee sit on the curb, splitting a bag of popcorn. Susie's not even here yet.

"Hey." Bert stands up when he sees me. "We saved you some popcorn." He holds out the bag, but Coralee walks a few feet away. "Excellent job on the Q and A. It was an unexpected question. I couldn't have prepared you better myself."

Coralee snorts. It sets fire to all the hurting parts of me. "What? You have something to say?" I shout so my voice won't break.

She starts speed-walking away from me, her arms pumping high and fringe swinging. I push past Bert and race toward her. She moves faster, but I easily match her pace. Doesn't she know she can't outrun a girl in a wheelchair? I roll up right next to her, so close we might as well be holding hands or throwing punches.

"Seriously, Coralee, you have something to say, spit it out or *shut up*." Saying it feels good-slash-bad—like picking a scab to watch it bleed.

She stops, and I grab my wheels to slow myself down. I take three breaths and turn to her.

She puts her hands on her hips. "You don't want to hear what I have to say, Ellie Cowan."

"I do *too*." I am not at all sure that's true. I'm raw and cut up inside from everything that's happened today—everything that's happened since Mom left, really. One more bad word from Coralee and I might not be able to put back the pieces. But we can't keep going like this either—tap-dancing around whatever "this" is that's wrong.

She yells, "You didn't even want to do this pageant!"

"I know!" I scream back, and it's like a dam bursting. "I did it for you!"

"So why are you trying to win it?!"

A kid passing by on a bike swerves at the sound and almost hits a parking meter.

"I'm not!"

Coralee lets out a totally cheerless laugh. "Yeah, right." She cups her hands under her chin and bats her fake eyelashes. "My mother is my hero. She made me everything I am. She is amazing and I am too."

She thinks *I'm* full of *my*self? If this is what happens when you let somebody into the deepest parts of your life, then I'm done. It hurts too much.

"It's not my fault your own mother can't be bothered to hang around." As the words spill out, I'm already trying to grab them back, but it's too late.

Coralee drops her hands and blinks like she's been slapped. Then, after a second where all I can hear is my own heavy breathing, she bends down so we are eye to eye. "I'm *glad* my mama didn't show up today, because she would have laughed her head off at what this pageant has turned into. It's just one big pity party."

"Shut up," I whisper, begging her in my mind not to say what's coming next, because if it's what I think it is, once it's out, we'll never be friends again. Ever.

"They only want you because you're in a wheelchair, you know," she says, and then adds, "I feel *sorry* for you."

"Shut. Up!" I scream. She narrows her eyes, and I know if I hear one more word I will lose my mind. I roll forward as hard as I can, my wheels aimed right at her kneecaps. She jumps aside one centimeter before we collide, and tumbles to the sidewalk.

"Are you crazy?" she yells up at me, brushing grit from her knees.

I turn away, so she can't watch me cry.

19

Self-Defense

Bert gets out of the Caddy at my house instead of letting Susie take him home. Coralee doesn't argue. She's all argued out, I guess. Who knew that was possible? The trailer is lit up like one giant firefly against the deepening blue of night, but I roll right past it.

He follows me down the drive, beyond the porch, and into the canning shed. The cool, wet earthy smell usually calms me. Not tonight.

"It's at least a mile to your place," I say.

"One point three, but yes"—he nods—"about a mile as the crow flies."

"You better get a move on, then."

I roll all the way to the back, away from him and the big Oklahoma sky. Everything feels too big right now.

"I heard you and Coralee fighting."

I turn around and try to read his face to see if there's judgment there. "All of Henryetta heard me and Coralee fighting."

"I mean," he says, brushing off some dirt from the cement blocks lining the shed. Then he sits down with his satchel perched on his lap, making himself right at home. "I heard what she said about them only liking you because of your wheelchair."

I close my eyes. "I really don't want to talk about it."

"For what it's worth, I don't think it's true. From an unbiased observer's perspective, I can tell you've formed some connection with the audience."

"Bert, you aren't unbiased. And it doesn't matter anyway, because I don't want to win!"

He cocks his head at me. "Then why are you so upset right now?"

Because my best friend thinks I'm somebody to pity. Because my dad hides out in the garage since he doesn't know how to talk to me. Because I miss my mom.

"Because Coralee screamed at me in the middle of the street."

"Did you know there's a type of tree in the rain forest called a sandbox tree?"

"Did you know that we *weren't* just talking about trees?"

Bert swivels his knees toward me. "It has spikes that run up and down its trunk to keep predators at bay."

"O-kay."

"And did you also know it's commonly known as the dynamite tree?"

"I did not."

"Because of its exploding fruit," Bert explains. "It's an incredible display of self-preservation, if you think about it. It senses danger and attacks."

I sit for a minute with that, staring past Bert through the doorway and into the yard.

"Is this your way of telling me that Coralee didn't mean what she said?"

Bert stands up and shoulders his satchel.

"Who said anything about Coralee?"

After Bert begins his 1.3-mile walk home, I know I should go inside. The boys will be waiting for me to say good night to them. But I can't face people yet. I back up to the wall and grab hold of the stretchy bands that Hutch tied to the shelf in the shed. Then I lock my chair and punch the air. Bert thinks I'm angry? He doesn't know the half of it.

Punch. Dad yelling at the boys to stop "roughhousing around Ellie!"

Punch. Rae Ann leaning over me, saying I have a "face for the stage."

Punch. Dad fumbling to make the lift work in the van.

Punch. Rae Ann putting her hands on my chair. Her face in my face. Her arm around my back.

Punch. Coralee on the sidewalk saying she feels sorry for me.

Punch. Rae Ann wiping a fake tear from her eye.

Punch. Dad turning his face away as he picks me up to haul me into the fishing boat.

Punch. Coralee basically ordering me to drop out.

Punch. Rae Ann telling the reporter that I am *so brave.*

I punch until my arms burn and my whole body quakes with tiredness. Hutch once told me that moving your body can be a way to ease your mind. But tonight, my thoughts are a knot that can't be loosened.

When I roll back toward the house with shaking arms, I spot Dad on the porch with two glasses of my sweet peach tea in his hands. I swallow a groan.

When I'm up on the porch, he holds out a glass for me and takes a seat. The rocking couch squeaks under his weight.

"Hey, kid."

"Hey." I sip the tea for something to do.

"Where were you off to all day?"

I open my mouth to tell him it's none of his business, but I'm too tired for my own attitude.

"I was at the pageant. You remember, *the one you told me I shouldn't do.*" Maybe not totally too tired. He stops rocking. "I forged Mom's signature and signed up. I know you don't think a person like me stands a chance, but I'm doing it anyway, because my friend"—I push past the word—"asked me to." I set the glass down. "And now I'm going to bed."

"Ellie," Dad says, shaking his head. "I don't— Maybe we should text your mother."

"Dad, no! I don't want to bother Mom. I've got this under control."

"But . . . a pageant? It doesn't seem like your kind of thing."

"How would you know what my 'kind of thing' is? You don't even know me!" I shout.

"I'm trying to know you. That's why I'm here!" He gets up and starts pacing the edge of the porch.

"Tell that to your *home office* in the garage." I squeeze out a laugh that hurts my chest. "You never wanted to know me. That's why you left. You couldn't handle the fact that I wasn't what you expected." I whisper the next words into my lap. "I'm the reason you and Mom got divorced."

I bury my head in my hands, but it doesn't block out the squeak of the rocking couch as Dad falls into it. He sniffs. I look up. His eyes are red when they meet mine. I've never seen him cry. I don't want to see it now. That's not how this works. He doesn't get to feel sorry for himself.

"Ellie, what happened between me and your mother—that was all me. If anyone should get the blame, it's me."

"I do blame you!" I shout. "But that doesn't mean it wasn't also about me." Why am I saying all this? I don't want to have this conversation right now. It's like the entire day has worn down the filter I have worked so long and hard to build up.

"I'm not good at . . . I'm not good at not being good at things," Dad says now, rolling the glass of tea between his palms. "Let us remember the fishing fiasco," he adds, but I don't smile. "I am built to be capable, Ellie. It's why I'm good at my job and run a 10K every year on Thanksgiving and always remember to set the coffee maker at night. But . . ." There is so much in that pause and I'm so worn out from this day, this whole month, that I'm not sure I can take whatever comes after it. Still, my body refuses to move.

"But everything about being your dad made me feel *in*capable." He looks up, and everything inside me crashes down. I wonder if he can see it on my face—the landslide that's happening inside. Or can you lose all hope without anyone ever knowing?

"You were so fragile for so long. Your mother jumped right in there, changing tubes, suctioning out your nose and ears when you got congested, massaging your belly and your legs. She was fearless. But me? I was terrified of messing up. Messing you up. It was a situation I couldn't fix. I thought"—he looks down at his hands and seems surprised to find the tea still there—"it would be better if I left."

"I didn't need you to fix me," I whisper, because I don't trust my voice. "I just wanted you to love me." And then I'm crying for real, the kind that feels like it will never stop, and I don't want it to. Because when it does, I'll have to face Dad again and all the other things he *needs* to tell me. I'm so sick of having to manage everybody else's feelings about me.

Before he can say more, I roll backward toward the door. "I can't—I can't talk about it anymore. Can we just . . . not?"

I don't wait to see what he says. It wasn't really a question anyway.

20

She's on Fire

You know what's underrated? Angry baking. Angry baking is the *best* kind of baking. I lay in the sewing corner for most of the night last night, going over everything that's happened since I let Coralee talk me into this pageant until my head throbbed and my back hurt and my heart ached. And then, sometime around sunrise, when the sky started its predictable turn from black to gray, I decided I don't *care* what anybody thinks.

Coralee thinks I'll win because of my chair. Dad thinks I'll lose because of it. But it's not about my chair at all. And it's not about them. Today I'm going to do what I do best: bake.

By ten a.m. the kitchen is a disaster of unwashed bowls

and broken eggshells and milk pooling on the counter. Every single dish we own is in the sink or on the floor. But I have managed to whip something up that will show them *exactly* what a showstopper looks like.

"Ellie," Dad says, coming in behind me with crater-sized shadows under his eyes. "Can we—?"

"Nope." I spin to face him. "No time to talk. If I'm lucky, I can squeeze in a shower and make myself presentable before you take me to the pageant."

"Me?"

I look around the hot, sugar-crusted, but otherwise empty kitchen. "Unless there's someone else in this room with a driver's license and time to kill?" I roll past him toward the bathroom. "And tell Meg and the boys they're invited too!"

We are in the Suburban, my brand-new dress fitting like a dream and my top secret dessert resting in a cooler by my feet, when I get a text from Bert:

Estimated Time of Arrival: Twenty-three minutes.

Bert *would* type out "ETA" and "23." I text back: Be there soonish. 1 more stop 2 go. And then I add a bunch of nonsense emojis to drive him crazy.

I called him earlier to tell him to go on with Coralee without me. I'd be hitching a ride with Dad. He didn't ask any questions. This is why I love Bert.

Before we've even come to a complete stop on Maple Lane, I throw open the Suburban's door. "You ready to rock and roll?" Mema and Grandpa are waiting on the curb in their Sunday best. Grandpa hitches his dress pants practically up to his armpits to climb into the front, and Mema tips her flowery straw hat to me. It's the first time I smile all day.

She taps my cooler with her toe. "This is what the secrecy was about?" I nod. "Then I wouldn't miss it for all the tea in China."

"Put your foot on it, Greg," Grandpa barks from the front as we exit Autumn Leaves at full speed toward the Rocking Horse Theater.

Dear Zoë François,

Your cookbook, Zoë Bakes Cakes, is one of the only actual cookbooks I own. Every single dessert is a work of art. I'm serious. I don't say that about every chef. But your Strawberry Charlotte Royale and Apple Butter Rose Tart are things of beauty.

So when I say that what happened today is not in any way a reflection on your craft, I mean it. I would not have done a single thing differently. Not one single thing.

With love and respect, your fan,
    Ellie Cowan

I smooth the collar down on my blue-and-white dress. Technically, the formal wear isn't until after the talent round, but I'm wearing it now because I'm not sure I'll get another chance and I want to enjoy it. Unlike every other time I have waited backstage, I am not one bit nervous.

"You look awesome," Maya says. She's not dressed up at all. In fact, she's the most casual I've ever seen her, in a T-shirt and ripped jean shorts. I don't get it until she turns to give me a hug and I read what's actually on her shirt. In big, bold letters it says:

Spelling is

~~DIFFACOULT~~

~~CHALENGENG~~

HARD.

"Nice," I say, giving her an extra squeeze before she walks out onstage. She grins.

I watch as the judges grill her for fifteen straight minutes on the trickiest words in the English language. She gave them the URL to the Scripps Spelling Bee archive so they could pick the best ones. When one of them asks her to "Please spell 'onomatopoeia,'" she rolls her eyes and orders them to choose something harder. They give up after she spells "gamopetalous" without so much as batting an eye. I'm not even sure that *is* English, but she bows and the audience applauds and she walks offstage beaming, so it must be.

As she leaves, I take a second to scan the crowd. Dad and Meg sit in the front row with Finn on Dad's left and Patrick on Meg's right. She calls it "safety seating"—as in "for the safety of all involved, you will sit as far apart as possible." I spy Bert on the aisle with Susie and Dane. He's taking notes. What could he *possibly* have to take notes about now? I keep scanning, but when I see who's on Dane's right, I gasp. Her hair is purple now, and it's pulled up in a ponytail so high the man with the video camera in the seat behind her has to crane his neck to see. But I'd recognize her anywhere. Coralee's mom. She actually came.

I turn toward backstage, searching the waiting area for Coralee, but I can't find her anywhere. I wonder if she knows her mom's here. And then I remind myself I don't care anymore what my former best friend does or doesn't know, and I face firmly forward. Turns out, I couldn't find her because Rae Ann was pulling her out onto the stage.

A spotlight opens on Coralee, who sports a jumpsuit the color of orange sherbet with a red belt and platform heels courtesy of Timeless Treasures. Her hair is curled out at the ends, and when she looks up, I note her glittery red sunglasses pulled down over her eyes. Here we go, then— the talent portion, Coralee's favorite part of the show.

Speakers crackle and piano music fills the auditorium. Coralee begins to sing. I've never heard the words to "Tiny Dancer" before. The fiddler only played the melody. But now, Coralee's low voice tells the story of a pretty-eyed girl, who everybody thinks they know and need something from. It's her. It's me. It's any girl who ever felt looked at but not seen. Halfway through the last verse, I wipe my eyes with the back of my hands. Dang it, Coralee.

She sings like her heart is broken, like shattered-plate, no-amount-of-glue-will-fix kind of broken. I want to roll out onstage and throw my arms around her, because that's what she'd do for me if I ever told her what I was actually thinking. I know she's feeling it too. I *know* it. Because that's how best friends work, even when they say the worst things and stop talking and one of them tries to run the other one over with her wheelchair.

But then . . . as the last chord fades and Coralee lifts her sunglasses, her eyes are dry. She's totally calm. She's got her game face on. I shake my head, angry at myself all over again. How could I forget one-third of Coralee's triple threat? She's an actress. And today, she even fooled me.

When she walks past me to the back of the stage, she flicks her hair toward me. It's all the motivation I need for what's about to come.

"And now, ladies and gentlemen, little misses and misters," Rae Ann announces, "please join your hands together to welcome Miss Ellie Cowan to the stage!" It takes all Bert's training to keep the smile on my face as I make my entrance onstage. But I hold it steady. Because I've got a cooler on my lap and a tiny bottle of Jack Daniel's in my pocket. I'm ready to roll.

"Hi. My name is Ellie Cowan, and my talent today is baking. I've been a home cook all my life, and it's what I love most in the world." I pause and look back to Coralee, who's hanging around the edge of the stage. "And it's what I do *best* in the world."

I pop the lid on my cooler, hoping my creation held up to the travel. I take my time unloading the ice packs. Rae Ann leans in a little closer as I gently lift the cake container from inside.

"And what tasty treat do we have here?" she asks, sticking the microphone right in my face. For today's festivities, she has chosen a skintight white ball gown. It's a miracle she can even bend at the waist.

"Well, Rae Ann," I say, giving her my best smile. "I thought that since this pageant has been around for so long and has *such* a history, I'd go a little retro and bake up a blast from the past."

I unsnap the lid and unveil my masterpiece—a rounded dome of creamy white that doesn't look all that impressive . . . yet. "This," I explain, gesturing with my free hand, "is a classic Baked Alaska, which I chose to fill with homemade strawberry, coconut, and blueberry ice creams to give it that special patriotic feel." I shoot the judges my best Coralee wink. Next to me, Rae Ann lets out a breathy *ooooooh* into the microphone.

"Many home chefs find the Baked Alaska to be intimidating—all that work to get the ice cream just right and whipping those egg whites for the fluffiest meringue only to stick it in the oven and pray you've got the magic formula of cold plus heat so it browns, but doesn't melt."

Rae Ann smiles so wide I can see a silver filling glinting from one of her molars. I bet you a million bucks and the Little Miss crown that she has never made a Baked Alaska in her life.

"But just because something has always been done a certain way doesn't mean it's the *best* way. Am I right?" A few claps break out. "One thing this pageant has taught me is that it's *never* too late to try something new."

Rae Ann beams. Somebody out in the audience yells, "Amen!" I palm the tiny bottle of whiskey. Mom would murder me if she knew I pilfered it from the wedding leftovers. It's now or never. "So, without further ado, I give you my Baked Alaska flambé!"

Before I can chicken out, I douse the meringue in whiskey, strike a match against the edge of my chair, and light the whole thing on fire.

Blue bubbles of flame burst over the white peaks, licking the edges and toasting the meringue a perfect golden brown. It's *marvelous*. A spectacle, just like I planned. The heat smacks me in the face and I lean back. But Rae Ann, poor Rae Ann, isn't quite as calm. I'm not sure how I expected her to react, exactly. But I did *not* expect her to shriek, cover her head with her arms, and then stop, drop, and roll away. I am left alone, center stage, with my blazing cake of glory.

For the safety of the general public, I dump a whole bottle of water over it, pick up the mic Rae Ann abandoned in her flight, and say, "Y'all enjoy the cake now. I quit."

21

Where's a Hallmark Card When You Need One?

"That was amazeballs!" Patrick yells when I roll down the ramp.

"Thanks, kid." I give him and Finn both fist bumps.

"Don't say 'balls,'" Meg orders, and gives me a squeeze.

On her other side, Grandpa's face is buried in a red handkerchief and his shoulders are shaking. *Please oh please don't let me have traumatized him.*

"Grandpa, you okay?" I ask, afraid to touch him in case he startles. But when he drops the hanky from his face, he is *laughing*, and then he gives me a fist bump just like the boys. "That's my girl, Ellie. Settin' the world on fire."

Mema steps between us and holds out her hand, palm up. I pass over the empty whiskey bottle and brace myself for a lecture. She leans over and whispers, "Best seventy-five dollars I ever spent," and gives me a wink.

Bert sidles up next to me. "That was both unpredictable and quite dangerous." Then he offers me his hand to shake. "But the crowd appeal was enormous."

I just quit, but I've never felt more like a winner. When Mom gets home tonight, she's going to be so mad she missed this. I'm still grinning when I see Dad over by the exit, leaning against the door and watching us. He catches me looking and waves me over. I try to hold the smile, but it slips as I roll to a stop a few feet away.

"Ellie, that was . . ."

"A disappointment?"

"I was going to say extraordinary." He runs his hands through his hair so that it shoots in all directions. "*You* are extraordinary."

Something a little like hope flip-flops in my belly. I shake my head. "Dad, you don't have to—"

"No. I wanted to say this last night but I didn't get the chance. Ellie, I love you so much. I don't tell you that enough. I owe you a lifetime of I love yous." He pauses long enough for me to hear the echo of all the unsaid words of love from all the years before. It almost hurts worse—the weight of getting what I wanted after I finally decided not to want it anymore. "And I'm sorry if I ever made you feel less than perfect. Because you are."

"Less than perfect?" I say, because I don't know how to feel now.

"What? No!" Dad yelps. "I was trying to tell you that you *are* perfect."

"I know." I paste on a smirk. "Because I'm also smart." Humor and baking. That's my one-two punch. If I had another cake, I'd light it on fire for distraction.

He squats so we are face-to-face and puts a hand on my shoulder. "Ellie, I've got to know . . . are you *trying* to kill me?"

"Not entirely."

"Seriously, though. I need to know you heard me. I love you so very much." He hugs me hard, like he isn't afraid I'm going to break, and that's when I do. I break wide open, and the hope inside me that things will be different, better now, busts out like a Roman candle. I smile into his shoulder until my cheeks hurt. But when he pulls back, I don't know what to do with my hands or my face. This is why Hallmark cards were invented. So people like me and Dad can share all the feels without the pressure.

"Thanks, I—" I fumble the words. "I know—"

He holds up a hand. "You don't have to say anything back. I just needed you to hear it." He grins at my relieved face and then rubs his hands together. "Now, do you want to get out of here? I have a feeling your mom is pushing all the limits on that RV to get back to you tonight. Unless . . . do you want to stay and watch the end? See how your friend does?"

As he moves out from the doorway, I see Coralee lingering near the exit not far behind him. She's supposed to be backstage preparing for her big formal-wear finale. Before the little sparkles inside me can fizzle out, I say, "I'll let you know in a minute," and roll over to her. She's still in her Elton John jumpsuit. She fiddles with the sunglasses in her hand.

"You didn't have to quit, you know," she says before I can open my mouth. "It'll suck the fun out of winning."

"Gee, thanks."

"What I mean is, you're pretty good at this pageant thing."

"Now I know you're lying." We're making small talk. It feels itchy and wrong, like accidentally putting on someone else's jacket when you expected your favorite hoodie.

She steps forward. "I'm serious. You know how to

work an audience. Bert can school us all day on the Rules and Regulations, but that kind of thing can't be taught."

"Well, I do have the whole 'pity factor' working in my favor, I guess," I say, and face the stage, where they are hanging bunting covered in stars and stripes from the rafters for the final round. I don't want to see her *I feel sorry for you* face again.

"I shouldn't have said that," she confesses. "It wasn't even true. I was just jealous."

"Liar," I say, with my back to her. But that sneaky hope is starting to glow again.

I turn back around and narrow my eyes. "*You* were really jealous of *me?*"

She studies her scuffed-up platform shoes. "Well, duh. Rae Ann was in love with you, and then you talked all about your mom during the Q and A and the judges *cried* and"—she clears her throat—"my mom doesn't even bother to show up half the time."

I cringe outside and in, hearing her say back to me almost the exact same words I said to her. It doesn't feel good to be right. "What I said about your mom . . . I'm sorry. Mema always told me nobody gets to judge a relationship unless they're swimming in its waters."

Coralee stops fidgeting but doesn't look at me.

"I'm real sorry. I am," I add.

"Yeah, well, you weren't wrong."

"She's here today, though, right?"

She doesn't answer, so I scan the crowd. But I don't see a purple ponytail anywhere. I roll closer to Coralee and nudge her toe with my toe so she'll look up.

"She *was*. With her new boyfriend, *Roy*," Coralee says.

I raise an eyebrow.

"They met this morning at traffic court. He restores cars over in Stillwater. She stayed long enough to borrow some money off Dane and then hightailed it out of here with Roy in his souped-up El Camino."

"That sucks." There are more words I could say, but none of them fix the particular disappointment a parent can cause, so I don't.

Coralee shrugs. There's a whole world of hurt in that gesture, but I can tell she's not ready to talk about it yet.

"I didn't quit the pageant for you," I say instead. "Just so you know. I quit for me. I'm tired of feeling like I have to do certain things or act a certain way just to make other people happy."

"You mean me?"

Do I tell her? We just made up . . . I think. I don't want to rock the boat. But I don't want that to be the way our friendship works now either, where we lie to make sure the other one doesn't get upset. It's not real if it's not honest. I go for honest.

"Sometimes, yeah. But I mean *everybody*."

"The pageant wasn't all bad, though, was it?" she asks after a beat.

"Nah. I got a great dress. And that Baked Alaska was once-in-a-lifetime solid gold."

We grin at each other and it feels good.

"You know," she says, pointing toward Rae Ann, who is smoothing her dress and chatting up the judges and seems no worse for her roll across the stage, "with the amount of hair spray in that updo, you could have set Rae Ann completely on fire."

I nod. "It was a risk I was willing to take."

She snorts. "I missed you."

"I missed you back," I say, and it's the truest thing I've ever said.

"Let's never fight again." Coralee bumps my shoulder. "At least until tomorrow. I want to win the pants off this thing first."

"Deal," I say, taking her camera from her and placing it around my own neck. "Now go make yourself the prettiest Little Miss Boots and Bows the world ever did see."

She drops into a graceful curtsy before sprinting off like it's the hundred-meter race.

"Take some good candids," she calls back, halfway down the aisle. "I need to update my portfolio!"

22

Hello and Goodbye

"**You're doing it all wrong,**" Bert explains to me, Coralee, and Maya as the sun begins to set behind the Dairy Queen. "To cover the greatest amount of surface area in the least amount of time, you have to eat quickly and in concentric circles."

"That's the dumbest thing I ever heard." Coralee bites off a chunk of chocolate-dipped cone. Half of it drips onto her silver strapless prom dress.

Bert points at her with his napkin. "See?"

It's the glowy twilight time that Grandpa calls magic hour, and we have the parking lot of the DQ almost all to ourselves, which is a blessed relief after the chaos and crowds of the pageant. Mom and Hutch are sitting inside, because as she put it, "I've had enough of the great out-doors for a while." But I don't mind the bugs or the heat if it means this night will last a bit longer.

My feelings over Mom finally coming home but Dad leaving are so complicated I'm not sure what to think about it. But I do know that when Mom leaped from the RV as we pulled in from the pageant this afternoon and ran across the gravel drive to tackle me in a hug, it felt like my heart beat normal for the first time in a month.

"Ellie," she whispered into my hair.

"Mom," I whispered back, breathing in the aloe and lavender scent of her.

She leaned back, but kept me pinned in her arms like she was afraid I'd disappear if she let go. "You're taller."

"You're *tanner*."

She slapped my arm. "Blame it on that guy, who insists that hiking is good for the soul." Over her shoulder, Hutch gave me a salute.

She gestured at my dress, the empty cooler in my lap, Coralee's camera still around my neck.

"You going to tell me what this is all about?" she asked.

"Eventually. You gonna tell me why I haven't been introduced to Beau Jr. yet?"

She dropped her hand from my shoulder and put it on her heart. "Els. About Beau—"

"Oh, *Mom*."

"It's not my fault! *No* one is meant to live in an RV for any extended amount of time, *especially* a fish."

We were both still laughing when Dad slammed the tailgate on the Suburban and came over to say goodbye. He stopped a few feet back from us. Mom dropped her hand and threw him her warmest smile. "Thank you for taking care of my baby."

"Anytime, Alice," he said, looking at me. This time I think he meant it.

"You are *all* doing it wrong," I say now to Maya and Coralee and Bert, biting off the bottom of the cone and sucking the creamy vanilla goodness through it like a straw.

"That is *genius*," Maya says, holding her own half-eaten cone up for inspection.

"No, you're the genius," Coralee says as Bert nods vigorously.

"You should have at least placed in the top three," I tell Maya.

She shakes her head. "My talents aren't the kind that win pageants."

"But they do win bees," Bert asserts. She throws him a winning smile, and he attempts to disappear behind his satchel.

"What even was that last word you spelled? Geo . . . gramo—" Coralee stutters.

"Gamopetalous," Maya answers, swinging her legs back and forth under the red picnic table.

"What's it mean?" I ask.

"It's an adjective used in botany to describe petals that are separated at the top but joined in the center." Coralee and I give her identical confused stares. "It describes something that might look different from one angle, but is actually the same thing at the core," she explains.

I suck on my cone again and think about Dad and Meg and Patrick and Finn on their way back to Nashville. And Maya about to head home, two towns over, where we won't have the excuse of the pageant to see each other every week. And Mema and Grandpa in their condo, hopefully sitting on their patio, watching the geese waddle around the pond. We were all smooshed together, a tangle of goodness, for one small patch of summer. Was it enough time for all of us to be connected in that way Maya's talking about—that deep-down, below-the-surface way?

I shake my head, lick my cone, and order myself to stop thinking. I just survived the Little Miss Boots and Bows Pageant. That's enough drama for one day.

Instead I reach over to touch the red sash pinned to

Coralee's dress. "I still can't believe you placed second. No way that baton twirler should have gotten first."

She turns to me and grins. "Are you kidding? That's the highest I've ever gotten! You sure you don't want to hit the pageant circuit with me full-time? You're my lucky charm!"

"I am not going to dignify that with an answer." I shove a napkin at her. "Here, you've got chocolate on your sash, Little Miss Runner-Up."

"Oh, that reminds me!" She hands Bert her cone so she can dig around in her purse. "Got you something."

I'm too busy wiping melted ice cream off my hands to see whatever she places on my head. It's so light, I reach up to check that there's really anything there. But when I feel the thin plastic, I know exactly what it is—the tiara from Timeless Treasures. Coralee holds up the camera, ready to snap a picture of me in my new favorite dress in the parking lot of Dairy Queen with a plastic tiara on my head and chocolate on my mouth. I have never felt more beautiful.

"Smile like you mean it!" she yells.

So I do.

Acknowledgments

Time to Roll **would not be here if it weren't for the** countless students and teachers and booksellers who asked after reading *Roll with It*: "But what happened next?" Of course, Ellie and her mom and Mema and Grandpa were still laughing and frying up fish and holding tight to one another in my imagination, but I didn't know if I had it in me to write a sequel. I didn't want to attempt it if I couldn't do them justice. They all, including sweet Bert and feisty Coralee, deserved the best continuation of the story possible. And then one day on a particularly hot run down the melting pavement in my neighborhood, the rest of the story just came to me—a neatly wrapped gift from the muses that started with a wedding and ended with a pageant. It was *perfect*. However, I wouldn't have been brave enough to tackle it without the support of Ellie's fans. So thank you, readers, for your voice that was louder than my fears. This story is for you.

Much gratitude also goes to my legendary editor Reka

Simonsen for indulging me in this venture and answering the email lickety-split that I sent while standing on the melting pavement after that hot run. I pitched this book in a flurry of excitement, and it was received with the same fervor.

Keely Boeving, my agent, also deserves a round of applause for diving into the pageant world with me and cheering on Ellie and Coralee in all their boots and bows.

I have always tried to honor and celebrate the differences in this world in how I live and what I write. My son, Charlie, has helped me tremendously with this as I attempt to fight for equality for him in school and the culture at large. And if I could pick a role model for him, it would be you, Katherine Beattie. You are tough and talented and funny and yes, whether you like it or not, a role model. Deal with it. Thank you for opening doors for kids like Charlie and for your friendship.

This sequel also allowed me to relive those extra special visits that I had with my grandparents as a child. Mema and PawPaw, I miss you still. I hope you are smiling and holding hands. I always think of you during the "magic hour."

Rae Ann Parker, thank you for letting me use your name for a character who couldn't be more opposite from you. You are kindness and compassion and always have your listening ears on, so of course it was fun to write your antihero.

Amy Marie Stadelmann, your cover illustration is epic as always. I only wish I had Coralee's jumpsuit and Ellie's smirk.

And Karyn Lee, you manage to make every one of my books a thing of beauty, so thank you for this and for all the ones to come.

I would also like to thank a particular bull in Colorado by the name of Beauregard, who enchanted my children and whose existence is legendary in our family. We still speak of you in whispers, and we wish you a longer life that Beau Jr. the goldfish.

Lastly, this one goes out to all the beauties in the world who don't think they fit in with the world's current trend. You do you. Sing, dance, roll, spell, bake to the beat of your own drum. You don't owe anyone anything. Love your own powerful self.